THE CASE OF THE

CASANOVA
CANTOR

THE CASE OF THE

CASANOVA CANTOR

an Augusta McKee mystery

Susan Moore Jordan

This is a work of fiction. All incidents and dialogue, with one exception, and all characters with the exceptions of historical figures are products of the author's imagination and are not to be construed as real. In all other respects, any resemblance to actual persons, living or dead, events, or locales is entirely coincidental.

The riot in Avondale, Cincinnati, on June 12, 1967, was an actual event, but the disappearance of a member of the Rockdale Temple staff is fictitious.

ISBN: 978-1-950625-28-4

Published by Shaggy Dog Productions, LLC

Library of Congress Control Number: 2023908865

Cover design and art by Taylor Van Kooten

(Back cover art inspired by Marc Chagall)

Books by Susan Moore Jordan

The *Carousel* Trilogy:
How I Grew Up
Eli's Heart
You Are My Song

Jamie's Children

The Cameron Saga:
Memories of Jake
Man with No Yesterdays
And This Shall Be for Music

"More Fog, Please"
(non-fiction)

Augusta McKee Mysteries:
The Case of the Slain Soprano
The Case of the Disappearing Director
The Case of the Toxic Tenor
The Case of the Purloined Professor
The Case of the Chrysanthemum Murders
The Case of the Unearthed Evidence
The Case of the 'Carousel' Killer
The Case of the Bogus Beatle
The Case of the Casanova Cantor

Table of Contents

To the music makers –
never stop connecting us
to the good in the universe.

Prologue
A World in Turmoil

Cincinnati, June 1967

The "long, hot summer" of racial unrest in the United States during the summer of 1967 exploded in Cincinnati's Avondale neighborhood on the evening of June 12. Tension had been building in the city since 1965, when the first in a series of brutal rapes and murders remained unsolved. The victims who survived all identified their attacker as Black, though none could identify him.

The situation came to a head with the controversial arrest and conviction of Posteal Laskey, the first viable suspect. Although he was convicted of only one crime, there were many who considered him the perpetrator of the others as well.

The community of Avondale, at one time predominantly a Jewish neighborhood, diversified as people from the Black community moved into the area. Soon enough, unfortunate tensions arose between the two communities. Many in the Black community felt Laskey had been railroaded. Following a tense but peaceful protest meeting that warm June evening, somebody threw a rock, smashing a window. Chaos quickly erupted.

Confirmation rehearsal had just ended at the majestic Rockdale Temple, now past its heyday as a showcase for Reform Judaism in the city. The young people exiting the building soon found themselves caught up in the disturbance.

Eugene Geller, the handsome and popular cantor for the Temple, along with several other adults—and with no little difficulty—managed to get the young people to safety. Once assured his charges were out of harm's way, Gene attempted to return to the Temple to pick up his car.

By then, the street fighting had escalated. Noise, objects, and smoke filled the air as members of the Cincinnati Police Department squared off against the rioters.

Gene did his best to avoid being caught up in the fray. In the confusion of the riot, he kept in the shadows, dashing toward a corner, rounding a building—and disappearing without a trace.

Chapter 1
A Prince Who Seeks for Truth

October 4, 1967

After a brisk walk around her Hyde Park neighborhood with Fritz, her three-year-old Golden Shepherd, Augusta McKee opened the back door of her comfortable Tudor home and brought the dog inside.

"Good Fritzy. Good boy." She rubbed his head, patted his flanks while unleashing him, and filled his water bowl.

Fritz had been a birthday gift to her husband, Lt. Malcolm Mitchell, Chief of Detectives of the Cincinnati Police Department. Dealing with a puppy had been something of a mixed blessing for Augusta, but the dog had long since become a source of joy to her as well as Mal. She now thought of Fritzy as her best buddy.

Augusta went upstairs to change into an outfit appropriate for attending the Rosh Hashanah service at Rockdale Temple, donning a wool blend dress in a soft dove gray with a straight skirt and matching designer jacket. Augusta had relished the early sixties fashions with swingy skirts and brighter colors. At five feet nine and with a model's figure, she could wear anything, and had begun to appreciate other new styles—to a point. She still favored her signature stiletto heels.

A tap at the front door, followed by her best friend, Millicent Devereaux, calling out, "We're here." Augusta had instructed Milly and her longtime fiancé, defense attorney Garrett Stoddard, to come in when they arrived and had left the front door unlocked for them.

She checked herself a final time in the mirror, freshening her powder and brushing back her chin-length chestnut hair, then headed downstairs to join her friends.

"You look incredible, as always," Milly said as she gave her friend a quick hug. "How do you do it? You don't age, you 'youthen,' like Merlin."

Augusta laughed. "Well, it's partly good genes, but mostly a lot of hard work. There's something to be said for 'aging gracefully,' even if I'm not quite ready for the aging part yet."

Garrett chimed in, "I find both you ladies lovely…each in your own way."

"Spoken like a true conciliator," Milly chuckled. "I take it Mal is still at headquarters?"

"He called about an hour ago and said something had come up and he wasn't sure when he'd be home," Augusta replied. "It would be great if it's a break in the Eugene Geller case."

"I said from the beginning I thought it was more than a missing person case," Garrett said, as he petted Fritz. "Not a trace of the guy, and it's been four months since he was last seen. His car is still missing, and he hasn't withdrawn a cent from any of his bank accounts. Nothing has shown up on his charge card. But of course, his body hasn't appeared, either."

"So you think he's dead?"

"Oh, Garrett always thinks that." Milly, a small, compact woman, fluffed her salt-and-pepper curls and smiled at her fiancé. "He's suspicious of everything. It comes from representing far too many killers."

Augusta glanced at her watch. "I think we have time for a quick glass of wine…or, Garrett, would you like a scotch and soda?"

Milly accompanied Augusta into the kitchen and the two women quickly returned with drinks. In Augusta's spacious, inviting living room, decorated in greens and blues, Garrett relaxed comfortably in an upholstered club chair with Fritz lying at his feet. The women settled into the roomy, foam green sofa.

"The police seem to have ruled out Geller being a casualty of the riot that night, because of the absence of a body," Garrett commented. "There's another theory floating around. It's rumored that Geller had a number of romantic assignations over the years, with at least one going on at the time he disappeared. It's possible he decided to take off with a new lady friend that no one was aware of. A way to avoid some of the complications he's had to deal with in the past."

Milly lifted an eyebrow. "That could account for the missing car, but what about money? That doesn't make a lot of sense."

"On the other hand, what better way to start a new life?" Augusta said. "Maybe he had a stash somewhere. Or this unknown paramour had cash. He could just become a new person someplace far away. Maybe Canada or Mexico. Or even Europe."

"Possible." Garrett, always an imposing figure in the courtroom with his military bearing and shock of white hair, finished his drink. "Ready, ladies?"

"I can't thank you enough for going with me," Augusta told them. "Mal's still uneasy about me going into Avondale, even though there hasn't been another outbreak of trouble since the riot in June. I hear the president of the Rockdale congregation is working closely with some of the Black community leaders, trying to keep things on an even keel until the building is closed."

"What a shame that has to happen," Milly commented as she collected their drink glasses. "But so many of the congregation members have already relocated out to Amberley Village, it makes sense that they would move forward with their plans to build a new temple there. I heard they already have the land they need."

Aware his mistress was leaving, Fritz curled up near the sofa in the living room as he cast her a reproachful look.

"Guard the house, dog," Augusta petted his head. "Daddy will be home soon."

***

Augusta McKee and Milly Devereaux had been best friends for decades, beginning in their undergraduate years at the Conservatory of Music more than thirty years earlier. After graduation, they spent three years together in Europe before returning to the U.S. where they were separated for a time. Milly married a doctor at Mount Sinai Hospital, a turbulent marriage that didn't last. She then lived for several years in California. A respected concert pianist, Professor Devereaux had returned some eight years earlier to join the faculty at the Conservatory, much to Augusta's delight.

After receiving her master's degree in opera performance from Indiana University, Augusta accepted a teaching position at the Conservatory. She remained single until she met then Homicide Detective Mitchell in 1963 when he was assigned to a murder case at Cliffside College, where she also served on the faculty.

Following a particularly contentious beginning between two strong-willed people, Augusta and Malcolm eventually found they enjoyed a mutual attraction…especially when Malcolm admitted he'd had a crush on Augusta when he saw her perform in *Carmen* at the Cincinnati Summer Opera, back when he was just out of high school.

That she was nearly seven years older concerned Augusta at first, but that concern was quickly laid to rest. They married two years later.

***

Augusta's primary purpose in attending the Rosh Hashanah service was to hear her voice student George Van Dorn sing the cantorial solos. When Eugene Geller disappeared, Rockdale Temple was left without a cantor. One of the rabbis took over some of the duties, but they needed an excellent singer to perform the High Holy Days music. George's family were members of the congregation and since he was now known locally as a promising singer, George became a logical choice.

"I know you're looking forward to hearing your boy sing the 'Avinu Malkeinu,'" Milly said. "He's really becoming quite a fine singer, Augusta."

"For a young guy who wanted to be George Harrison of the Beatles not much over a year ago, he's really settled down. He's impressive, Milly, and he sets an example for my other students. Between you and me, he's one of the reasons I've selected *The Magic Flute* for the spring opera production. At this point, his voice is perfect for Tamino."

Milly nodded. "And we have that transfer student who is an excellent coloratura who can be your Queen of the Night."

"Yes, Angelica Costa. She's had fine teachers, but I'm glad she's here. Claudia Prince really knows how to bring out the best in coloraturas."

"We're fortunate that Claudia is still teaching at the Conservatory. I know she's had offers elsewhere," Milly observed.

"That's all very nice, Augusta, but your kid George can't fill the hole Gene Geller left at Rockdale Temple forever. He's got his future to consider," Garrett said as he pulled into a parking space.

The air had cooled after the sun set, and it was a crisp, pleasant evening. Augusta glanced around as the three of them walked the half block to the Temple. It was something of a shock to see a couple of what had been thriving businesses still showing damage from the rioting. *It seems quiet here, but I'm glad I'm with Milly and Garrett. You can sense tension just beneath the surface in Avondale these days.*

They arrived at the Temple and entered the imposing Romanesque building, once the pride of the Reform Jewish community in Cincinnati. Letitia and Harold Van Dorn spotted Augusta as she entered and rushed to her. As always, Letitia was dressed in her unique style of colorful prints and flowing floor-length fabrics.

"Oh, you did come!" Letitia exclaimed, embracing Augusta. "George hoped you'd be here. He's so thrilled to be singing tonight."

Augusta introduced Milly and Garrett to the Van Dorns and the three of them joined George's parents in their family pew in the sanctuary. Letitia handed them each a service book, and the music began.

The music throughout the service was particularly beautiful, as Augusta had expected. When George sang the prayer to "Our Father, our King"—the "Avinu Malkeinu"—the congregation listened attentively. It thrilled Augusta to hear how his voice filled the sanctuary. His clear, strong tenor suited the haunting melody perfectly, and he sang the prayer with reverent expression.

The choir was situated in a balcony behind the Ark of the Covenant, and after the service ended Augusta and her friends waited to speak with George. He flushed with pleasure as he watched them approach.

"You were absolutely stunning," Augusta told him. "I've never heard the 'Avinu Malkeinu' sung more beautifully." Milly and Garrett added their praise, and George beamed at all of them.

"I can't thank you enough for coming," he said, as Letitia and Harold stood to one side, proudly gazing at their son.

"At Monday's lesson we'll be starting on a new aria," Augusta said. "Mozart."

George's eyes shone. "'Dies Bildnis'? So, are you planning for *The Magic Flute* to be the spring opera production? I've been listening to Fritz Wunderlich's recording. Man, he was so, so good. I'll be ready."

Returning to Garrett's car, Augusta felt slightly uneasy, but the congregation seemed to be making their way safely from the Temple. She noticed two beat cops on the other side of the street, two more about a block away, and she also spotted three patrol cars as they drove through Avondale.

"I see the CPD is keeping an eye on things," Garrett commented. "Jake Schott doesn't want any more trouble in his city."

"I guess having a new chief has been an adjustment for the police department," Milly observed. "But I know you said Mal and Chief Schott are good friends."

"Apparently, everybody on the force loves Jake," Augusta replied. "It was a pretty smooth transition after Stan Schrotel retired last January."

Augusta found Mal waiting at the door when she entered their house. As always, her heart fluttered at his greeting. She still thought him the most handsome man she'd ever seen—tall and trim with dark hair and intense blue eyes. A warm kiss and embrace, and she sighed and relaxed in his arms.

"So how did George do?"

"He was wonderful. He should be perfect for the role of Tamino in *The Magic Flute*." She glanced around. "Everything all right here?"

"Yes, fine. Fritz greeted me when I came home. He's been out and is set for the night." He took her hand and drew her into the living room where they sat together on the sofa.

"I have some interesting news, Gus. I believe Eugene Geller's body has been found."

Chapter 2
Of Evil and Good

Augusta removed her jacket, kicked off her stilettos, and settled back to hear what Malcolm had to say.

"Survey team plotting the route for Interstate 71 was just finishing up for the day, and they found something damned unusual. Human remains. They had been there long enough to be degraded. Found in an obscure area and obviously there had been animals about."

Augusta cringed. She'd had her own experience with bones, but those had been buried in a neighbor's backyard for decades when Fritz dug one up during the replacement of a patio. A human heelbone. This sounded much more grisly.

Mal observed her closely. "Do you want me to skip part of this?"

"No, I want to hear it all."

"What they found was mostly bones. Some were missing due to the animals having uncovered the corpse in a shallow grave." He paused.

"You know, I think I could use a glass of wine," Augusta stood. "Do you want anything?"

Mal pulled her back down. "I'll get it. Sauvignon blanc?"

"Yes, please."

Augusta sighed and relaxed against the sofa. *Bones again. Merciful heavens. But these could be the bones of someone I actually knew.*

Mal returned with glasses for each of them and regained his seat.

"So, the head of the survey team immediately contacted his boss and was told to stay put. Of course, the police were called and very quickly two beat cars and a supervisor arrived on the scene. The supervisor contacted Homicide, even though there wasn't any way to tell what had caused this person's death. The situation called for it." He took a healthy swallow of wine.

"Danny was one of the detectives who responded to the call," Malcolm added, referring to his younger son who had followed in his father's footsteps.

"I remember what happened when Fritz dug up that bone in our neighbor's yard," Augusta said. "But this was a much different situation, so I assume there may have been an even closer inspection of the scene?"

"Yes, they canvassed the area for any evidence of anything. Identification, evidence of dragging, any articles of clothing or other personal possessions. They made note of missing bones. They even collected soil samples in a few locations."

Augusta sipped her wine, and Malcolm again observed her closely. "You sure you want to hear all this?"

"Of course I am. You know me. Living with a detective is catching." She chuckled nervously. "I need to hear everything."

"Danny then instructed one of the patrolmen to secure a Workhouse crew. Boy, that's a job and a half...what those guys have to do."

"You mean prisoners serving time in the Workhouse have to come out and collect the...remains?" Augusta drained her wineglass and handed it to Mal, who raised a finger.

"Hold that thought." He quickly strode into the kitchen and returned with the wine bottle, refilling Augusta's glass and his own.

"What happens next is that Communications will dispatch a patrol wagon to pick up a crew of the more docile, less escape-risk prisoners who can volunteer for this detail. In exchange for that, those prisoners' time can be reduced by a few days."

"Because it's an awful job. Go on, I'm listening. Sounds gruesome."

"Well, they'll have a body bag, and they'll be wearing gloves...and maybe boots. They'll do the best they can to get the...mess...into the bag, and place in on the floor of the truck. Then they'll have to sit on the benches in the truck and try to find someplace to put their feet."

Augusta poured herself a third glass of wine.

Mal lifted an eyebrow. "You said you wanted to know the details."

"I know I did."

Mal leaned an elbow against the back of the sofa and rested his chin on his hand as he grinned at her. "You'll like this part. Best case scenario, the patrol wagon driver will be an old codger. He'll drive to a liquor store on the way to the Coroner's Office and buy his detail some wine or whiskey. It's against the rules, of course, but the Workhouse is aware the prisoners will come back drunk."

Augusta had to chuckle. *Mal is so matter-of-fact.*

"I think I know what happens next. They'll deliver the body to Gary's office," Augusta said. Gary Ridgeway, the Hamilton County Coroner, was a personal friend of Augusta's, as well as a fellow musician. "And the body will be placed in a refrigerated drawer until Gary gets in the next day…which means tomorrow…to perform the autopsy."

"You remember how that goes," Mal said. "And now you know more than you ever wanted to know about what happens when a body is found that could be a recent victim."

"Why do you think this is Gene's body?"

"The time frame is right. He's been missing for about four months. His killer was sure the body would never be found, not even thinking about the possibility a survey team might venture into that area." A final swallow of wine. "Danny felt pretty sure it was the body of a man and he thought the same thing I did, the missing cantor. He'll be back over there in the morning once

Gary has completed the autopsy. And I'll be there as well."

Mal stroked Augusta's face. "Are you going to be able to sleep?"

"Yes, I'm fine. But you're absolutely right...sometimes I ask too many questions. What a picture I have in my head right now."

Mal kissed her softly. "I'll bet I can get those images out of your head."

"I have no doubt you can," Augusta said as she returned the kiss.

***

Both Danny Mitchell and his brother, Ryan, were Mal's sons from an earlier marriage which had ended when Carla decided she didn't like being married to a cop. That she had met her second husband before ending her marriage was something Mal never spoke about, but Augusta knew it had been hurtful. However, Malcolm and his ex-wife had agreed then to maintain an amicable relationship because of their boys.

Ryan, now a successful attorney in a prestigious law firm in Cincinnati, had married Lacey Stevens, a stunningly beautiful brunette actress with a promising future who performed at the Parkside Playhouse. Danny's wife Martha had been one of Augusta's most gifted students throughout her college years. Augusta believed Martha had all the tools: a fine, naturally beautiful voice which she used with expression and expertise, the intellect to learn accurately and quickly, and a passion for music. Topping it off, a pleasing stage appearance—trim, but with a womanly figure, and blond hair and blue eyes. What was always an unknown for an aspiring performer was how much luck they might have.

Martha seemed determined to pursue a career in opera until she met Danny. As much as she loved performing, she had opted instead to make her life with her now-detective husband, and to limit herself to whatever singing engagements became available in and near Cincinnati. She seemed happy with her decision, and they now were the proud parents of a five-month-old baby boy named Malcolm. At his grandfather's suggestion, the family agreed to call the baby Max.

Augusta had not spent much time around babies. She was an only child whose mother had died during the 1918 Spanish flu pandemic, and her deceased father had few family members. So spending time with little Malcolm was an entirely new experience for Augusta.

The first time she held Max at the hospital, Augusta felt unbelievably awkward. Malcolm sensed her unease and relieved her of the burden fairly quickly.

Later at home, he addressed the situation. "No babies in your background, I take it?"

"No, none. I apologize if I made you uncomfortable. But no siblings with children, no close friends…I mean, Milly has been my closest friend for decades, and neither of us had children. Sometimes my former students show up at school with their new baby and I always admire it from a distance. They're sweet, I'm sure. But they're so…helpless, so fragile. I don't know how mothers do it."

Milly laughed heartily every time they discussed Augusta's new role as a step-grandmother.

"Somebody is going to drop him, and I don't want it to be me," Augusta had said after that first meeting before Max was taken home.

"Nonsense, you won't drop him. You might clutch him too tightly, though. There's an art to holding a baby."

"And you're an expert because…?"

"A bunch of cousins with babies. I babysat numerous times when I was out in California with that part of my family. Don't forget, we all started out the same way. Even you."

"I was never that helpless," Augusta said firmly, to Milly's hoot of laughter.

"Fortunately for you, you don't remember it. What is your earliest memory, anyway?"

"Dancing around my living room when I was three or four. I insisted my father allow me to take ballet lessons about that time."

"You started bossing grown men around at an early age, Augusta."

As the months passed, little Max began to smile and make enchanting baby sounds. Next he seemed to study faces and recognize people, and then began reaching for hands and toys, and Augusta found she enjoyed being part of his life. Watching him develop became a fascinating process, and she especially loved seeing Malcolm with this child he adored.

Milly happened to stop by one day in September to find Augusta babysitting Max with no sign of anyone else on hand. She fed the baby as he reclined in an infant seat which she had placed on the table in the alcove, a soft towel draped over one shoulder to wipe up whatever needed wiping up.

Milly watched admiringly for a few minutes. "You've come a long way. Look at you feeding the little nipper as if you know what you're doing."

"This is kind of fun. He loves peaches." Augusta offered Max another spoonful, which he eagerly chomped.

Milly checked the tray of baby food on the table. "Yes, well, I see he's also supposed to be getting peas."

"He hates peas. Martha can feed him those if she really thinks he needs them."

Milly guffawed. "Well, I can see in a few years Maxie will know exactly who the pushover in his family will be when he wants something."

Augusta dabbed the baby's mouth gently with the towel. "He really is a beautiful child. Look at those blue eyes. Just like Mal's."

Milly laughed and shook her head. "Who would have ever thought it? Augusta McKee, opera singer, renowned teacher, lauded stage director, honorary detective…doting grandmother."

***

The day after Eugene Geller's remains were found, Augusta tried not to dwell on that event and instead think about the good things in her life. She was admiring the sweet little baby blue coat and cap she'd recently bought for Max when the phone rang.

"I thought you'd be interested to know this," Mal said. "It can't be confirmed until Gary reviews his dental records, but it definitely seems the body found yesterday is Eugene Geller's. Right height, and the amount of time the bones were out in the elements seem to confirm it. Cause of death: a bashed-in skull."

"Well, the last time Gene was seen was after that confirmation rehearsal at Rockdale Temple, and his car still hasn't been found. Hmm, it's unlikely a rioter would have gone to all the trouble of moving and burying the body. So it seems to me the killer knew Geller would be at the Temple and took advantage of the chaotic situation."

"Good work, Detective Gus. That's what Danny and I came up with. Somebody who had been looking for a way to do away with him. Who knows…the killer may even have been the person who threw the rock that caused all hell to break loose."

Augusta returned the jacket and hat to the gift box. "So what happens next? You start looking for suspects? And I'm sure Gene's wife Elena will be the first person you talk to."

"The spouse always has to be eliminated, you're correct. And she may have had a good reason to want to be rid of him."

"I can't see Elena doing anything that violent, Mal. She seems like such a sweet, gentle soul. Of course…she could've had someone working for her…or with her. But she's been putting up with his escapades for so many years it's hard to believe she would end up resorting to violence. Why not just divorce him?"

"She certainly seemed upset when the missing person case went cold and was closed. Of course…her reaction is what we'd have expected. We'll certainly take a good look at her."

Malcolm paused. "And husbands and boyfriends that Gene possibly cuckolded will have to be considered as well. We've got a lot of investigating to do on this case."

"Don't forget about the women he had flings with. I know of one woman who was heard to say she'd like to kill him."

"Yes, the ladies, too. 'Oh, what a tangled web we weave…,'" Malcolm quoted. "Sounds like a scenario right out of a bad soap opera. Well, I'll provide my homicide detectives with whatever assistance they need."

Augusta smiled. "I'm sure you will." *And probably go a bit above and beyond with this one,* she thought. *This is a big case. No way will Mal be able to leave it completely in the hands of his homicide detectives.*

Chapter 3
Reaching for the Light

Saturdays Augusta had no set routine at the Conservatory, but she sometimes scheduled makeup lessons or meetings. On this particular Saturday after Rosh Hashanah, she had a meeting with Dean Dale Williamson to discuss her opera production scheduled for early March. She planned to hold auditions soon and have a few rehearsals before her cast members became busy with the Conservatory's winter vocal ensemble activities.

As always, she would expect her cast to work on learning and memorizing their roles on their own. Once school resumed in mid-January after the winter break, rehearsals would begin in earnest during the weeks leading up to their March performance dates.

After the racial uprising in Avondale in June and the continuing tension there—which likely would heighten when the news of Gene Geller's murder was released—Augusta had begun to wonder if there was any way music might be used to help settle the unease in her city.

She didn't know that she as an individual could do much, but she did know one thing which had troubled her for several years: some of the finest singers who attended the Conservatory had in the past been denied the opportunity to appear onstage in an opera production. While a few Black students were now participating in opera workshop, none had performed in leading roles. Augusta believed it was time for that to be addressed head on.

"Why do I have an idea what you have on your mind, Augusta?" the dean asked, once they were seated comfortably in chairs in his office.

"We've discussed this before, Dale. It's unconscionable that the fine Black singers who attend this school don't seem to have the same performance opportunities others do. Nobody ever talks about it, but it's a fact. It's past time for Cincinnati to move into the present. Marian Anderson first appeared at the Met in 1955, and Leontyne Price is—and has been for several years—one of the star sopranos there and internationally."

"It hasn't been an easy journey for Price. She's met opposition in numerous ways."

"Yes, I know. All the more reason for us to move forward, to help ease the way for upcoming Black opera singers however we can."

"I suspected your choice of opera had something to do with dealing with local social problems. And the fact that you've chosen to perform *Die Zauberflöte* in English, rather than in German. You announced it as *The Magic Flute*."

Augusta sat forward eagerly. "Mozart was nearing the end of his life when he wrote his allegorical opera, and he wanted to make a strong statement about his beliefs. He believed in searching for truth and enlightenment, love and reason. Honestly, what better way to present these than disguised as a fairy tale?"

Dale drummed his fingers on his desk. "You're thinking we live in a time when we could use some reason and enlightenment, I'm sure."

"Could we ever. Of course, nothing will be decided until my staff hears auditions, but George Van Dorn is definitely a candidate for Prince Tamino. I wish you'd heard him sing at Rosh Hashanah the other night. Very impressive, and very moving."

"Two other important casting requirements for this opera, though, are Sarastro and the Queen of the Night." Dale ticked them off on his fingers. "Sarastro, who needs extreme low notes, and the Queen, who sings in the stratosphere. I believe this opera contains the lowest and highest notes performed in any opera."

Augusta nodded. "True, but happily Allan Meissner is back working on his masters' after his service in Vietnam. He has the low notes, and is certainly an imposing figure on stage. Also, we have a strong coloratura who can handle the Queen of the Night."

"You mean Angelica Costa. Yes, I would think she'll be chosen for the role. And it's great to have Allan back. I was kind of surprised he was accepted into the military because of his height."

"He's six feet six. The maximum height is six feet eight. I'm grateful he made it back safely and returned to the Conservatory to resume his studies."

Dale steepled his fingers. "All three of these singers are white, but I think I know where you're headed. Denise James?"

"Yes, Denise James. She's a strong possibility for the role of Pamina, the Queen of the Night's daughter. She's blossomed over the past two years and I think has a potential opera career ahead of her if she continues to do the good work she's been doing. She's in the ensemble in the workshop production currently in rehearsal, but Denise is more than qualified for a leading role."

"And you think you might cast a Black soprano opposite a white tenor for the leads in *The Magic Flute?*"

"If Denise is chosen by the audition board for the role of Pamina, I want to feel I can offer it to her." Augusta clasped her hands together. "Her race shouldn't make any difference, but it would be unrealistic to not acknowledge there could be opposition from some people in the community, regardless of what's going on in Europe...and in New York."

She drew a deep breath. "Frankly, I believe the majority of our students would be very happy to see this happen."

Dale leaned back against the chair and stared at the ceiling. "Using a fairy tale to break the color barrier...not a bad idea at all."

"Well, if I have you in my corner, I'm willing to discuss this with the Board of Directors if you think that's necessary."

"I'm definitely with you on this. Let me think about how…or even if…we should involve the Board."

"Oh, good," Augusta stood. "I'm going to announce auditions for the week after our opera workshop performances."

They walked to the door together.

"I'm excited to do this opera, and I have a lot of ideas…thanks to the composer." Augusta gazed at Dale. "Most people have no idea what a remarkable person he was. Mozart certainly showed us that with his final opera."

***

Once an imposing Victorian mansion, Main Hall housed offices and a reception hall used for performances on the first floor, and private studios on the second floor. Knowing that Milly was usually in her studio on Saturday mornings, Augusta climbed the curved mahogany staircase and leaned against the door as she tapped it.

Milly immediately opened the door and Augusta nearly fell into the room. "I figured that was you. I saw your car when I parked a few minutes ago," Milly told her. "You cornered Dale about your thoughts for the Mozart opera, I take it?"

"I did. Of course, I assured him I wouldn't 'pre-cast' the opera…on the other hand, we never select an opera unless we know we have the students who can sing it."

Augusta strolled to the large window which looked out over the front of the campus, a charming view with its curving driveway, stand of large trees, and small garden. "He agreed this would be a perfect opera for a racially mixed cast. I'm thinking of Denise James as a possible Pamina, of course. And John Edmanston has a young Black baritone who I think is auditioning for Papageno."

"The Bird Man"? Milly laughed. "Well, Mozart included fanciful characters in this opera, so I'd think you can just enhance that."

"The other thing I like—the opera is full of hope. We need that right now in this city…well, in this entire country."

"You don't think all the Freemasonry stuff might be a bit much?"

"Oh, I think Mozart soft-pedaled that by making his opera a fairy tale." Augusta turned away from the window and moved to the settee in Milly's spacious studio. "And what can possibly be bad about an allegory that basically presents the ideas of tolerance and respect for others, concern for the community's needs, and the pursuit of truth?"

"That's true," Milly agreed.

"And Mozart and Schikaneder wove a wonderful tale and created intriguing characters."

"How can you even remember the librettist's name?" Milly asked.

"I've been practicing it," Augusta said, airily. "Then Wolfgang topped off his fairy tale with some divine music."

"If anybody can pull this off, it will be you," Milly said. "And I'll do whatever I can to help." She seated herself at the piano and began cleaning the keys with a soft cloth.

"Well...looks as if you're expecting a student, so I'll get out of your hair." Augusta turned back before she left. "We need to go to Meck's soon. It's been ages."

Milly grinned. "Yes, it has. I could do with some good sauerbraten."

Augusta decided to stop at Mecklenburg's Beer Garden on her way home for takeout, in hopes Malcolm might have returned from his office in City Hall by the time she reached their house. The popular German restaurant had opened sometime in the 1890s and was a staple in the city. Over the years, it had become a favorite gathering place for musicians after opera performances at the Zoo, and the two couples often met for a meal in the outdoor garden during mild weather, enjoying being in the open air under entwined grape vines illuminated by lanterns.

Augusta picked up two schnitzel sandwiches and fries, along with some of Meck's famous pickles, and arrived at her house to see Malcolm just getting out of his car.

"Perfect timing," she said as she kissed him.

"You stopped at Meck's?" He grinned in delight. "I knew there was a reason I married you."

Mal took Fritz out for a quick run as Augusta set the table and opened beers for both of them. While she generally preferred wine, schnitzel sandwiches definitely were meant to be paired with good beer, and Mal had four bottles of Guinness he'd been saving for just such an occasion. While Augusta wasn't much of a beer drinker, she did enjoy a Guinness, especially with Irish or German food.

"What a nice, unexpected treat," Mal said as he joined her.

Augusta gazed around the room, one of their favorites in the comfortable house. The alcove was part of an addition to the house some years after its construction. A spacious kitchen, a pantry which now served as Fritz's "holding tank," and this airy, pleasant room. The outside wall consisted mostly of windows overlooking Augusta's garden, and the door opening into the dining room was glass as well, so the room had a spacious feeling.

They took most of their meals in this room as the dining room also served as a music room, and housed the small grand piano Augusta had purchased along with the house. The former owner had been a member of the Conservatory faculty who used the room for private recitals and musicales, and for a time Augusta had done so as well.

When she bought it, the house had seemed too much for one person, but when Malcolm came into her life, she realized it was perfect for the two of them. Augusta wondered at times if she'd had some kind of odd premonition that she might finally meet the man of her dreams and that was one reason she purchased it.

Mal wiped his mouth and hands, dropped his napkin on his plate, and stood to take their dishes into the kitchen. "I'm going to have another Guinness. Would you like one?"

"Thanks, save it for yourself. As much as I enjoy an occasional Guinness, they tend to make me sleepy."

She smiled as she heard him washing the dishes in the kitchen sink without even mentioning it to her. *That's the kind of marriage we have*, Augusta thought. *We look for ways to make each other's lives easier.*

She joined him in the kitchen, and when they were finished, they moved into the living room and settled on the sofa as Mal sipped his drink.

"What can you tell me about Eugene Geller?" He asked. "We can't start interviewing people until we have a positive identification from his dental records, but Danny and Jim are putting together a profile as best they can." Jim Edmonds had been Malcolm's partner as a homicide detective, and now was senior partner with his son.

"They have his dental records?"

"It's routine to request them in a missing person case, so yes, Gary has them. At this point it's more a formality than anything else because we're all sure it's Geller."

Augusta said over her shoulder as she went into the kitchen, "I think I will have that last Guinness."

She resumed her seat next to Mal, kicking off her stilettos and tucking her feet under her. "Eugene

Geller—everyone called him Gene—graduated from the University of Cincinnati probably in the mid-forties. He was a business major and a music minor and studied voice with John Edmanston, so I was acquainted with him. But he didn't take part in opera workshop or in the major opera productions."

"I'm told he was an excellent baritone. You may have been the person who told me that, in fact. And I'm pretty sure Milly was the one who told me he was 'gorgeous.'"

"I can hear Milly saying that," Augusta laughed. "I never thought of Gene as 'gorgeous,' not movie-star handsome. Of course, my personal standard of male beauty runs to ruggedly handsome men like the hunk I was lucky enough to marry."

Malcolm grinned his appreciation.

"But Gene had something. He was a good-looking guy, to be sure. Dark hair, big dark eyes, a charming smile that often seemed to melt women's hearts. More than that, Gene was very conscious of his appearance. You never saw him in anything except a freshly pressed shirt. Hand-tailored suits. Yet he managed to always appear casual. And he was a genuinely nice guy…except of course for that roving eye. Which may have turned out to literally be a fatal flaw."

Augusta smiled. "He indeed had a fine baritone voice. As I recall, he had been the cantor and choir director at Rockdale Temple probably from the time he was in his mid-twenties. Some Reform synagogues are hiring fulltime professional cantors these days, ordained after years of study at the seminary, people who have many clergy as well as singing duties. I think Gene would be more accurately described as a paid cantor soloist and choir director. He graduated from U.C. and walked into a cushy job in his father's brokerage firm, but stayed on as cantor at the Temple."

Mal nodded and finished his Guinness. "Geller Financial Services. Which Eugene's father inherited from his old man."

"Gene and Elena married young; I think she was twenty-one. He was a couple of years older because of his time in the military. They had their first child within a year or so. As I said, this is just what I've heard. I first met Elena somewhere...maybe a fund-raiser for the Conservatory or the Summer Opera. And I've seen her several times more recently, since her oldest daughter attended Cliffside."

"Attractive woman. There are four children, as I understand. Jim had some information he shared with me...the Gellers were separated twice during their marriage, most recently about three years ago."

Augusta gazed at her Guinness. "I can't finish this. I'm going to fall asleep sitting here if I try."

Mal laughed and reached for the bottle. "I'll help you with that." He took a sip and lifted an eyebrow. "And help you upstairs if and when you'd like."

Augusta stretched out, arching her back. "Why not? Sounds like an ideal way to end the afternoon to me."

"Before I get too distracted, what were you saying about Geller?" Mal asked, gently rubbing her shoulder.

"The rest is hearsay, and you've probably heard the same things I have about his extracurricular activities.

No doubt that was what prompted the separations. I'll talk to Milly, she seems to be a gossip repository."

She suddenly sat up straight. "Oh, one thing that may be important. I mentioned a woman who said she'd like to kill Gene? His sister-in-law Amanda, Elena's older sister. And I heard that more than once."

Chapter 4
Past and Present Dangers

"You remember I said Milly is a 'gossip repository?' Well, another one is the Cincinnati Revolver Club, if you happen to be around at the right moment."

Not long after Augusta was kidnapped by a member of the criminal element in Newport, Kentucky, Malcolm had suggested she learn to use a revolver. She resisted for a time, but had been skilled as a skeet shooter as a youngster, and eventually began lessons at the Revolver Club. Her skills adapted easily to shooting a pistol. She also found she enjoyed it and went to the club at least once a week for target practice.

Augusta leaned forward. "That's where I heard about Amanda Weatherly having it in for her sister's wayward husband. And the women who were talking about it were also expressing their admiration for Amanda as a crack shot and a woman who seems to be completely fearless."

"Go on." Malcolm examined the Guinness bottle.

"Apparently, Amanda is an expert marksman. She's hunted game in Africa and elsewhere. Both her children have learned to shoot." She paused. "One more thing...her son recently applied to the CPD police academy."

Mal thought for a moment. "With those credentials, I'd say it's highly unlikely she would have killed Gene by bashing his head in."

"On the other hand, with those credentials, she might have known she'd be an immediate suspect if he'd been killed by a gunshot."

Mal grinned. "My word, Professor McKee, you do think like a detective."

"I've been told that before," Augusta smiled. "If I think of anything else about Amanda, I'll let you know. I've never met her. But I thought you should know about her threats, since she doesn't fall within the considerable segment of the female population whose hearts Gene Geller has allegedly broken."

"Anyway...what was that plan we had again?" Mal pulled her to her feet. "Going upstairs for some reason?"

He gave her a lingering kiss. "And I have the day off tomorrow. The entire day."

***

"Yes, I'd heard that about Amanda Weatherly," Milly told her on Monday. Augusta had arrived at the Conservatory early to speak with her. "Another person I have to wonder about is Dolly Booth."

"Oh, I can't believe she'd harm a hair on Gene's head. She seems to be madly in love with him, and has been for years."

"To the point it's suspected two of her six kids could be Gene's. Maybe Dolly wouldn't want him dead, but what about her husband, Leon? He has to wonder about those two dark-haired children he supposedly fathered."

"Well, that can happen. Recessive genes and all that...no pun intended," Augusta smirked.

"Aren't the blond, blue-eyed genes the ones that are recessive? But I guess a mixed gene pool would explain it...actually, it's not that unusual."

"I'll tell Mal and he can pass it on to Danny and Jim," Augusta commented. "That's going to be tricky, though. What reason could they give for bringing Leon Booth in to talk?"

"I'm sure they can find some reason. Maybe just that they're talking to people who knew Gene," Milly replied. "For background."

"I know they sometimes do that, but Leon would probably immediately know they were aware of his wife's relationship with Gene, don't you think?"

She paused, her hand on the doorknob. "Well, that's for them to figure out. In the meantime, I've got an opera workshop production to get on stage next week."

When first offered the position of Director of the Opera Department the previous year, Augusta had given it careful consideration, wondering if it would overwhelm her already busy schedule. She now realized she relished the responsibility, grateful for the team she'd assembled to make sure all productions—whether a complete production, as with the spring opera, or the "op shop" performance—came off with as few hitches as possible.

The usual programming for opera workshop presentations consisted of two shorter, sometimes one-act, operas or selections from two full-length operas. Augusta liked coming up with a common theme for the evening of opera to be presented to the public.

John Edmanston, former director of the Opera Department and a colleague whom Augusta considered her mentor, was still on the voice faculty at the Conservatory and had agreed to share directing duties with her for this fall production. They had opted to present an evening of fantasy. John's assignment was selections from the second act of Rossini's opera *La Cenerentola*, based on the Cinderella story. The second half of the production would be the first act of Offenbach's fantasy *The Tales of Hoffmann*, performed in English, which Augusta was directing.

Her entire directing staff was on hand for the rehearsal this afternoon: John; the conductor Byron Matthias, also on the Conservatory faculty; rehearsal accompanist Miriam Levengood; and Stacy Mathis, their choreographer, from the dance faculty. This was a first production for Miriam and Stacy, and Augusta found them enthusiastic and more than capable.

She looked over her notes as she watched the *Cenerentola* rehearsal, pleased that John continued to be active. He had always been a first-rate director, but failing health had prompted him to begin handing the reins of the department over to Augusta during recent years.

After a fifteen-minute break, the *Hoffmann* cast took the stage. Augusta had given them basic blocking at the previous rehearsal. Today, they would try it to see how well it worked, making whatever changes were deemed necessary.

Angelica Costa, the coloratura Augusta felt sure would win the role of the Queen of the Night in *The Magic Flute*, was a perfect Olympia, the live doll with whom Hoffmann fancied himself in love. She had been experimenting with "doll-like" movements even during some music rehearsals. For this rehearsal, she tried different movements and expressions enthusiastically, to everyone's delight. More than once the cast was convulsed with laughter and the rehearsal came to a halt.

Pleased, Angelica glanced around at her castmates and gave Augusta an innocent "What did I do?" look.

"It's fine," the director told her cast. "Get it out now. You can't respond like that during a performance. But Angelica, what you're doing is absolutely perfect."

Augusta made some changes in staging as they worked, and the corrections seemed to make the production flow more smoothly. Once set and props were added, more adjustments might need to be made.

Listening to George Van Dorn's singing confirmed to Augusta that his fine tenor voice was beginning to open up as she had been sure it would. Singing the entire role of Hoffmann would not have been possible for George at this point in his life, but the lyrical singing in the first act suited him well. Augusta was even more pleased to see how believably he acted the role and how comfortable he was on stage. *He may make it,* she thought with a smile.

It's hard to believe it was only last year that he went through a traumatic experience because he wanted to be another George Harrison, she thought. George bore a resemblance to Harrison, and showing up at a Beatles' concert in Crosley Field dressed as his idol had led to George actually being mistaken for Harrison and kidnapped. *The good news is the experience resulted in him focusing on the career he realized he really wanted, singing opera.*

Because Augusta had been instrumental in winning George Van Dorn's eventual release from his kidnappers, an even stronger bond now existed between teacher and student. He hung around a bit longer than the rest of the cast after they were dismissed.

"So...I love singing this music, Professor," George said. "What do I need to work on to make it better?"

How nice to hear that from a kid who at one time slid by, doing as little as possible. "You're singing well. Keep reminding yourself to never push high notes."

"Was I doing that?" George looked slightly stricken.

"No, not at all. As I said, just a reminder. Your upper register is very beautiful. It can be a temptation to want to make your high notes bigger, and it's not necessary."

"Got it. Don't 'oversing.'" George smiled warmly. "Can I help you with anything? I'm not in any rush to get anywhere."

"No, but thank you for asking," she returned the smile. *Yes, he's come a long way.*

Augusta placed score, notes, and other items into her briefcase and headed for her car. She had one other singer in mind for a possible leading role, Denise James. She'd recently had a visit from Denise's father Arthur, who shared some concerns with her, and she recalled their conversation as she drove home.

"Professor McKee, Denise has always loved to sing, and my wife and I have encouraged her and we've done what we can to give her music lessons."

Mr. James sat on the edge of the chair, dressed in what Augusta suspected was his best suit, hat balanced on one knee. "We live modestly. I work for the postal service and appreciate the salary and benefits, but we don't have a lot extra."

He leaned forward. "My wife Debra is a fine seamstress, and she brings in some extra money by sometimes doing alterations or making a garment for one of her customers. Denise's choir director in our church gave her piano lessons for free, and even found a piano to give us. She recommended a voice teacher for Denise, someone who had once studied here."

"Yes, I know Denise's first teacher. She's excellent, and gave your daughter a solid foundation. It's one reason Denise won a scholarship when she applied here."

"Denise is our only child. We'd been saving for college since she was a baby, so with the scholarship that hasn't been a burden. But our idea was always that she would study music education and become a teacher."

"And that was how she first matriculated here, Mr. James. But when she came to me and wanted to switch her major, I encouraged her. She told me her dream is to sing opera. And honestly, I believe she might have a shot at doing just that."

He looked at the floor. "This isn't easy to ask. From what I've read, there aren't many African American opera singers around. Especially not in this country." He paused. "And it seems like those who are singing opera have to go to Europe, where they have more opportunities. That takes money we don't have. I don't know where that could come from."

Augusta stood and walked around to the front of her desk, leaning against it. "Mr. James, the fact is, most opera singers have to spend some time in Europe, no matter what their ethnicity. Opera in Europe is an established part of the culture. People there love opera, and they...even the young people...will buy tickets to see operas. Nearly every city in many countries has an opera house which employs singers. Provides them with a salary and benefits." She smiled. "In fact, some large European cities even have more than one. There are three professional opera houses in Berlin."

Arthur stared at Augusta, moving his hat nervously to the other knee. "You're telling me, it's a job? I guess I didn't know that, but it makes a big difference. I don't like to think of Denise going so far away from home...but I want my daughter to be happy. But how could we ever afford to send her to Europe?"

"There are foundations in this country, some right here in Cincinnati, that provide money to promising singers. Most are grants, which generally do not have to be repaid, unlike loans. And there are competitions that award cash prizes. It's not easy for any singer, but it can happen." She paused. "One thing you should be aware of—as good as Denise is, there are many others who are also special. And one important element in all this is that we have no control over who gets the breaks."

"You mean which singers will be lucky."

"Yes, that's exactly what I mean." Augusta paused. "Perhaps I should have contacted you before encouraging Denise to change her major. If this has become a problem, I sincerely apologize."

"No, Professor McKee, Debra and I agreed to let her try. I'm glad you've given me all this information, though. It's great to know she can apply for financial help if she really wants to be an opera singer. Denise seems to have her heart set on it."

With this conversation in her mind, Augusta made her way home through the pleasant streets of Hyde Park to her house. Cincinnati is a city made up of distinct neighborhoods, and the Hyde Park neighborhood consisted of comfortable older homes built on larger lots. Augusta didn't like the word "opulent," but no doubt some people thought of her part of the city in that way. She wondered where the James family lived. *Mt. Auburn? Walnut Hills? Maybe South Avondale?*

Augusta considered herself fortunate to live where she did, and undoubtedly the unrest in the city had made her, and many others, more aware of the sometimes vast differences among the neighborhoods.

She had never thought of herself as an activist but believed strongly in people being appreciated for their ability…for their talent. It seemed in her world of music that was generally accepted. But society had some catching up to do, in her opinion. And if she could help with that, she would.

Malcolm's car wasn't in the driveway yet, so Augusta returned Fritz's greeting at the door and took him to the back, putting his leash on to take him for a walk. They went around the circle, past the house where not many years before she had been held captive by a member of the same crime family whose members had kidnapped George Van Dorn the previous year.

Her captivity had been brief and was far enough in the past for her to be able to shake off the slight uneasiness Augusta felt as she approached the house. She had been happy when it was sold. The children playing in the yard waved at her and called out greetings to Fritz, who picked up his ears and wagged his tail in response. Augusta waved back and continued her walk to her house.

Oh, good, Mal's home. She and Fritz went in through the back door to find Malcolm putting water in the dog's bowl.

After an embrace and a kiss, Mal followed her into the living room with a happy Fritz at his side. "I brought the mail in," he commented, relaxing on the sofa, stretching out his legs and draping his arms across the back.

"Thanks." She picked it up and flipped through it.

This is odd. A letter-sized envelope with her address printed in all caps, no return address, postmarked Cincinnati.

Augusta opened it and read the brief message.

A chill ran through her. She sank onto the sofa next to Malcolm, handing the note to him wordlessly.

BE CAREFUL WHO YOU CAST
IN YOUR OPERA

Susan Moore Jordan

Chapter 5
The First of Three Ladies

Mal took the note carefully and studied it for a moment. He pulled a handkerchief from his pocket and held the paper in the cloth, carefully refolding it. He used the same handkerchief on the envelope as he replaced the note, and it startled Augusta to realize he was doing this so as not to smear any fingerprints. He then wrapped the envelope in his handkerchief and placed it in the inside pocket of his jacket. *He's taking this seriously*, she thought.

"Have you talked about your ideas for casting the spring production with anyone other than the dean?"

"Only Milly, but I'm sure you knew that. I think most of the students are aware of my wish that we had cast Black students in the past. I know they realize we have some outstanding Black singers presently studying here."

"I'm going to hang onto this." Mal frowned, patting his chest. "I'm sure if you have any other such missives…or if anyone says anything out of line to you…you'll let me know."

"I need to fix something for dinner." Augusta stood. "I'm afraid I've lost my appetite, though. I didn't expect something like this, and maybe I should have."

Mal wrapped her in his arms and held her close. "It may be nothing. Let's get out of here and go someplace for dinner." He pulled back and gazed into her face. "How about Lenhardt's?"

Augusta sighed and snuggled closer. "Actually, that does sound good. Let me freshen up while you feed Fritz and I'll allow you to sweep me off my feet."

The popular Viennese restaurant in Clifton proved to be only moderately busy, and they were seated promptly by their usual server, who greeted them warmly. Lenhardt's was another favorite eating place of Augusta's and her appetite had more than returned when their dinners arrived.

"Any progress with the Eugene Geller case?" she asked, savoring her Italian schnitzel.

"Only that Gary confirmed the identity of the body the survey team found."

Mal paused. "Oh, here's an interesting piece of information…Elena Geller didn't report her husband missing for over a week. She was in Colorado with her children and when she didn't find him at home when she returned, she contacted his co-workers and asked if they knew his whereabouts."

"That does sound odd," Augusta said. "She was out of town for over two weeks and hadn't even talked to him? What was she told?"

"His secretary said he'd taken some time off, so no one at the firm was concerned." Mal eyed Augusta's plate. "Do you need that little piece of schnitzel?"

"It's yours," she chuckled. "Why didn't you order this if you wanted it?"

"Because I wanted sauerbraten more and figured my lovely bride would share her food with me."

"We really have become an old married couple," Augusta said. "You're so sweet to call me bride when I'm now a...," she took a sip of wine and swallowed, "...a grandma."

"Forever youthful, and forever my bride," Mal responded, resting a warm hand on hers.

"And you're forever my wonderful detective and my groom."

Mal lifted the hand and kissed it. She gazed at him for a moment, then said, "So tell me more about Elena."

"When she reported Gene missing, she was questioned rather closely because of the lapse in time. It had been over a week since anyone had seen him."

"Well, when it's an adult, that's not too unusual, is it? Isn't there a kind of 'waiting period' before the police get actively involved?"

"Yes, that's the way it's handled. Quite different for a child, of course...including a teenager. But adults...sometimes people want to get away, for a variety of reasons."

Augusta pushed food around on her plate. "Something else. Is there any way of knowing when Gene actually died?"

"Gary has estimated a three-week window from the last time he was seen, which was the night of the Avondale riot. But with the remains so degraded it's difficult to come up with an exact, or even approximate, date."

Mal leaned back and stared at his wife. "Honestly, Gus, it's pretty incredible you can be sitting there enjoying your dinner and talking about this. I think I've been a bad influence on you."

Augusta observed the bite of food on her fork. "Well, before I became involved with you, Detective, I doubt very much I'd have been having this conversation during a meal. But you've let me into your world, so here we are." She grinned and took a bite. "And oh, this is so good. I believe it's referred to as 'compartmentalizing.'"

Mal laughed and shook his head. "If you say so."

"Back to Elena, though," Augusta said. "How long had she been in Colorado? And she took her kids? She couldn't have left more than a week prior to the riot because of school."

Mal swallowed the bite he'd been chewing. "She was visiting a cousin in Boulder, and actually took the younger kids out of a school a couple of days early. It did seem surprising she hadn't at least talked to him once during the two weeks she was gone."

"Unless she was considering separating from him again," Augusta mused, gazing at her wine glass.

"How well do you know her?"

"Her oldest daughter just graduated from Cliffside. Elena's family are staunch Roman Catholics, and she raised her kids in the church. Gene even went to services with them. He may have considered converting at one time if I remember correctly."

"Did her daughter study voice with you?"

Augusta shook her head. "No, but you saw Cathleen onstage in your favorite Gilbert and Sullivan operetta."

They smiled at each other, recalling their first meeting of four years earlier when Augusta directed *The Pirates of Penzance* and Malcolm had solved the mystery of the murder of a student while Augusta continued preparations for the show. Though an opera lover, Malcolm had initially declined to watch *Pirates* because he questioned the way the police were presented, but he eventually attended the final performance. And the night following that performance was the first time they were together as lovers.

"Well, Elena Geller has a fairly solid alibi. Out of town with her children visiting relatives the day he was last seen. And she did report him missing the day after she returned. So that pretty much eliminates her...though she could have hired someone to do away with him."

"I can't see her doing that at all. Whatever Gene's failings as a husband, everyone agrees he's a great father to their kids. For that matter, he's—he *was*—a great second dad to all of Dolly Booth's children. By the way, Dolly's husband Leon has moved out. Not sure if he just learned the truth or threw in the towel."

Their server stopped to clear their plates and take dessert orders. After he moved away Augusta said, "I've told you about Elena's sister Amanda, who openly hates

Gene. It's been a source of contention between the two sisters and Elena and Amanda barely speak."

"We need to take a close look at Amanda, then. And interview Dolly and Leon Booth, as you suggested."

"Together?"

"Not at first. Individually. Dolly as someone we understand was close to Gene. Leon so we can figure out if he knew about his wife's relationship with the victim."

Augusta nodded. "Those discussions should be interesting."

Mal grinned at her. "Looking for puzzle pieces, Detective Gus. You know the drill."

Augusta was quiet on the drive home.

"Try not to think too much about your anonymous letter. It could very well be a one-time thing and that will be the end of it," Mal suggested.

"You and I both know that might not be the case," she replied. "First of all, the only people I had talked to were Milly and Dale. So why would anyone even mention it?"

"You're a pretty outspoken lady," Mal said. "You may have mentioned in some kind of social gathering that you'd like to see the Conservatory using more diversity in casting its productions. And your new position is now public knowledge."

Augusta considered this. "All of that is true, and yes, I've spoken my mind more than once about former Conservatory students being overlooked. And the upcoming opera production is the first one I'll be solely in charge of. No doubt I'll be under a microscope."

Mal put his right arm around her and drew her close. 'You've got this, Augusta. The dean told you he's behind you and I'm sure the majority of the board of directors will feel the same."

"And best of all—I have you in my corner." She sighed and kissed his neck.

***

Augusta had completed her final lesson for the day and began preparing for her opera workshop rehearsal. She responded to a tap on her studio door to see Elena Geller, appearing agitated and slightly unkempt. A very pretty woman and usually carefully groomed, her generally well-coiffed hair appeared unruly, and it also seemed she hadn't given much thought to matching jacket and skirt when dressing.

Poor woman. She's just learned her missing husband was murdered. "Come in, Elena."

"I hope this isn't a bad time, Augusta." Elena pushed her blonde hair back from her forehead as her eyes darted around the room.

"Actually, it's perfect timing. I've completed my lessons for the day and have some time before an opera workshop rehearsal." Augusta extended a hand. "Please…sit down."

"I'm sure you know about Gene." Elena's voice shook.

"Yes. I'm so sorry for your loss. It must have been a horrible shock to learn of his death."

"The thing is…how much do you know? The police aren't telling me hardly anything. I mean, I kind of had accepted that he was…wasn't coming home, ever, but when they showed up and told me his…his remains…had been recovered, they didn't add much information."

She shifted in the chair and crossed her legs. "Then they asked me a bunch of questions about where I'd been and why I hadn't reported him missing sooner. I'd answered the same questions already, so I started to feel like a suspect or something."

"They were just doing their job, Elena," Augusta soothed. "It was a shock for them to find Gene's remains the way they did. They very much hoped to track him down and return him to you alive and well."

Elena snapped open her purse and flicked out a handkerchief, dabbing her eyes. "Well, yes, I understand that, but why grill me like that? As if I may have had something to do with…with his death?"

"Sadly, when someone dies under suspicious circumstances, the first thing the police do is eliminate the spouse as a suspect. It seems brutal, but it's necessary. I'm sure they tried to question you as gently as possible."

"It didn't feel that way to me." Elena sighed heavily and twisted the handkerchief.

"No doubt it did not," Augusta commiserated. "And I wish I could tell you more, but first of all, this is not Malcolm's case. And even if it were, he couldn't confide any details about his investigation to me." Augusta's fingers were crossed behind her back. *Not always true,* she thought.

"Elena, the police will stay in touch with you and keep you apprised of their progress. I can promise you that. I know you and your children have a lot to deal with right now. Why not focus on them and not worry about anything else for the present?"

Another deep sigh. "I'm sure you're right." Elena stood. "Well, thank you for talking with me, Augusta. I'm on my way to the funeral home to make the arrangements...I loved him, Augusta. I always did, and I hoped...." Her voice trailed off as she appeared to struggle to control her tears.

"I can't imagine how difficult this is for you, Elena. Again, I am so, so sorry this happened. Gene was a wonderful father, and I'm sure your children are a great comfort to you and to each other."

Augusta gently walked her guest to the door. "I'll watch for the announcement of the service and will certainly try to be there."

She closed and locked her studio and headed to the Recital Hall for the opera workshop rehearsal, putting aside her questions about Elena and trying to focus on the task ahead. Today it was only her *Hoffmann* cast on call, to have a double run in order to polish their performance.

The dancers were on stage as she entered and Stacy finished her rehearsal with them, ready to work their performance into the act. Byron, the conductor, stood behind Miriam at the piano, checking through the dance music to be sure his tempos were in agreement with Stacy's.

What a relief to be here, Augusta thought. *This Gene Geller murder is hitting too close to home.*

During the break she gave the cast, Augusta glanced around, observing how the students gravitated toward each other. Denise and George were at the center of one group, and Denise seemed comfortable with her friends. *No overt signs of racism here,* Augusta thought.

But regardless of Mal's telling me not to worry about that piece of hate mail, I can't ignore it. Not with this city—this country—on the edge of turmoil.

Chapter 6
The Second of Three Ladies

After rising early the next morning, Augusta headed for the Cincinnati Revolver Club for some target practice. Through a window, she spotted Elena Geller's sister, Amanda Weatherly, shooting.

Interesting how little the sisters resemble each other, Augusta thought. Elena, blonde and curvaceous; Amanda, dark hair cut short, lean and angular.

Augusta stood near the window to watch and was impressed with Amanda's skill. She never missed a target, and they were moving toward her at high speed. She'd heard of Amanda's prowess as a marksman but it was something else entirely to witness it. Amanda completed her session, removed the ammunition clip from her pistol, and took off her ear protectors, preparing to leave. Augusta would be next to use that lane.

Amanda strode from the range and spotted Augusta. "I know you," she said, staring at Augusta with a piercing gaze. "You're the voice teacher from the

Conservatory who is supposed to be a crack shot. You know you're kind of famous around here, don't you?"

"No, I hadn't heard that." Augusta fought back a laugh and extended her hand. "I'm Augusta McKee. I've certainly heard about your skill, Mrs. …Weatherly."

A brief, strong handshake. "It's Miss Weatherly…but just call me Amanda. I kept my maiden name even when I was married. Something I believe you've done as well." This last delivered with a bit of a sneer.

Ignoring the remark, Augusta replied, "I'm glad to meet you, Amanda. I don't know about being a crack shot, but I've found I enjoy using my pistol for target practice."

"And you're married to a cop…rather, to the man who is now Chief of Detectives. My son Atticus is applying to the Police Academy for next year."

"Well, I highly approve of his choice of profession. Some of the best people I've ever known are in law enforcement." *Where's this going, anyway?* Augusta wondered.

Amanda moved toward the locker room, turning her head back as she said, "His choice; certainly not mine. Oh, and tell your husband to get his detectives to back off, will you?"

Somewhat distracted by the encounter and especially by Amanda's final remark, Augusta's session was not her best. She returned to her house to change for her day at the Conservatory, took Fritz outside for a short walk, and drove across Madison Road. *"Tell your husband to get his detectives to back off."* It sounds as *though she's been subjected to some intense questioning. So she's definitely a suspect.*

On arriving at the Conservatory, Augusta decided to talk with Milly since she had a half hour before her first student.

"Do you know Amanda Weatherly at all? I met her at the Revolver Club just a while ago. She's…unique."

"So what did she tell you?" Milly grinned. "'Unique' is a good word. I think Amanda got married so she could have two kids because she dumped her ex-husband about a year after her daughter was born. A son first. Two years apart. Of course, if she didn't have an inheritance, she couldn't have had the lifestyle she wanted as a divorcee."

"You're saying the Weatherly family is wealthy? I hadn't heard that before." Augusta perched on the edge of the settee and Milly joined her.

"The fact that there's a lot of money in our city seems to be a well-kept secret for some reason. Yes, an ancestor of Amanda and Elena's back in the nineteenth century was a beer baron, as I understand it."

"So the husband was just a means to an end—giving her children. Not ever a love match."

Milly nodded. "It's well known how much she hates…hated…Gene Geller. She never felt he was good enough for Elena. And I'm sure the police must consider her a suspect, just as you and I have."

Augusta repeated the parting remark Amanda had flung at her. "It sounds as if the police have questioned her more than once. Even though I understand she also was not around on the twelfth of June. Off somewhere in Africa on safari with her kids."

"I've met Atticus and Autumn. They're actually quite nice young people."

"So their initials are all A.W. Another way to declare they're all hers?"

"The 'single parent' to the 'nth' degree, maybe. I don't know when they see their father…or even if they ever do." Milly moved to her piano and began to sort through music.

"She sounds even zanier than Letitia, George Van Dorn's mother, only in a different way." Augusta shook her head. "Letitia is flaky, but she's sweet. And she's harmless. Amanda, maybe not so much of either of those. But she obviously considers herself a 'modern woman.'"

Augusta stood and moved to the window. "What happened in Avondale in June…and what's going on all over the country…I hardly recognize this country sometimes."

"It's the sixties, Augusta," Milly said. "Cincinnati is a conservative city, but elsewhere all sorts of strange new things are going on. You know that. People are experimenting in all kinds of ways."

Augusta replied, "What's that saying? 'Tune in, turn on, drop out'?"

"Timothy Leary, and his experiments with psychedelic drugs." Milly sat and played a few measures of a song. "It's the Cole Porter song come back to life, 'Anything Goes.'"

"Porter wrote that musical right at the end of the twenties. Are we reliving the twenties? I always thought the 'Roaring Twenties' happened as a reaction to Prohibition."

"Yes, but don't forget that the twenties also followed the horrors of the Spanish flu pandemic and the Great War. Can you imagine what a relief it must have been to have survived those two disastrous events? Women's fashions back then certainly reflected a sense of freedom...possibly because of women finally being given the right to vote. There's a bit of that same trend today, because of the feminist movement. But if Amanda Weatherly is a 'modern woman,' she's a very unpleasant one."

Milly eyed her friend. "You know, Augusta, what you're wearing today could be a modified 'flapper' dress."

Augusta glanced down at her new dress, a wool blend in forest green with a soft flair to the skirt, three-quarter-length sleeves, non-existent waistline. "You're right, it could. I like the styles we're enjoying these days."

"How much shorter are skirts going to get?" Milly asked wryly. "Nice color for you, though. It brings out the green in your eyes. I'll bet Mal loves this one."

Augusta grinned. "Yes, he does. But you'll never catch me in go-go boots—I'm sticking with my stiletto pumps."

Milly abruptly stood and looked at her watch. "This has been a fascinating discussion, Augusta." She grinned. "We both seem to have a grasp on what's going on in this complicated world...but I have a student coming in ten minutes. Can we take a rain check on the history lesson?"

"Of course," Augusta chuckled, "though it's been fun. I have students all afternoon as well. Thanks for filling me in on Amanda Weatherly and her kids."

***

Augusta's final lesson was George Van Dorn, who had prepared "Dies Bildnis" as his audition for *The Magic Flute.* Observing his performance, Augusta couldn't help comparing this confident young man to the kid who'd been so enamored of the Beatles that pretending he was George Harrison placed him in a complicated, dangerous situation just last year.

At the same time, she understood his fascination with the "Fab Four." His undeniable resemblance to Harrison resulted in George Van Dorn for the first time in his life being considered attractive by females. She had recently overheard one female student describe him as "hot." *Just look at him now, this poised, extremely attractive young tenor, singing with such expression and beauty of tone. He has a lot going for him—and I doubt he wants for female companionship. I guess he IS 'hot.'*

The last note faded. "Beautifully performed, George. I think you should do a strong audition. And remember—you'll be auditioning for the audition board, not just for me. And I know you understand I'm not listening to you as my student, but as another singer auditioning for a production that I'm stage directing."

"I know, Professor McKee. We all know how productions are cast here and how much you respect your colleagues."

George lingered for a moment after Augusta's student accompanist left the room. "Of course, you know how much I'd love to sing this role." He hesitated.

"Something else?"

"I hope Denise James is being considered for Pamina. I'd really love to perform with her."

"You also know I never pre-cast a production, George. Obviously, we select an opera, or even scenes from an opera, because we know there is more than one student capable of singing each role. I believe Denise is one of several sopranos who could perform Pamina."

"Professor McKee, I'd like to address this head-on." George drew a deep breath. "Will Denise being Black be a factor in casting the opera? I sure hope not. And I want you to know I've talked to my parents about this, and they feel the same way."

"First of all, it will not. And secondly, thank you for telling me about your parents being supportive."

George gazed at her. "Well, I will be, too, whether I get Tamino or not. We all know some people may not like that kind of casting. It's about time people in this city realized that in Opera World, what matters is talent. Period."

What you don't know, George, is that people 'not liking that kind of casting' has already started with a nasty, anonymous note I received. Well, let's hope that was a one-time thing, and that's the end of it.

Augusta nodded. "Noted. Good lesson today."

She cleared off her piano and closed the lid on the keyboard, gathered up her score and legal pad covered with notes about *The Magic Flute*, and went to meet with her production team. What she had reminded George of was true. Each member of that team would be present at auditions, and each had input. The final decision was Augusta's, but it pleased her that there was seldom any disagreement about which singers were best for which roles in the opera.

She headed for John Edmanston's spacious studio for the meeting. Along with John, the other members of the audition board were Stacy and Byron. Some people were surprised she included her choreographer in making casting decisions. But Augusta had always seen opera as a multi-artistic endeavor. Yes, paramount was the sound, the music. Yet opera was also visual, and how people moved on stage made a difference in the audience's experience.

Augusta thought this particularly true of *The Magic Flute*. She believed Mozart wanted a feast for the eyes as well as the ears in his fantastic allegory.

Stacy ran to catch her as she crossed Highland Avenue heading for West Hall. "This is exciting, Augusta. I'm honored to be part of your staff for your first production as chair of the opera program."

"An important part, Stacy. I'm going to want these singers to move more than they generally do onstage."

The two women joined their colleagues and got to work.

***

To Augusta's surprise, Mal's car was in the driveway when she arrived home. And it was even more of a surprise to walk into the house and be greeted with the aroma of Italian food.

Mal stood in the alcove doorway. "I stopped at LaRosa's. Hope you're okay with Italian tonight."

"You are the very best, Detective." She kissed him warmly. "I meant to say 'Lieutenant.' Old habits die hard, you know."

He returned the kiss. "How was your staff meeting?"

"It was excellent. I'm excited about putting this production together." She paused. "Oh, I met Amanda Weatherly this morning. Elena Geller's sister. Interesting lady."

Mal gazed at her. "I have other things on my mind than the Geller case. I'd prefer no shop talk tonight."

Augusta caught something in his expression. "What's going on?"

He sighed and leaned against the door frame. "A pretty tense racial incident today near Walnut Hills High School. Fortunately, it was successfully defused. But you're right about the ongoing uneasiness in our city, Gus."

Augusta put her arms around him. "I'm so sorry, Mal."

"So am I. I'm sure it won't be the last." He hugged her hard. "Anyway…Fritz has been walked and fed, so the evening is ours, bride. Can we make tonight only about us?"

"That sounds perfect to me." She kissed him again. *Whatever I can do to ease your distress, my dearest love.*

Chapter 7
The Third of the Three Ladies

"The reason Amanda Weatherly has been interviewed several times is because she lied to us about being in Africa on safari on June twelfth. She didn't even leave the country until the fourteenth." Mal refilled his coffee mug. "She's tough, and she's minimally cooperative. And she's also smart."

"So she's still a suspect," Augusta commented, sipping her coffee. One sugar, two splashes of cream. Try as she might, she was unable to drink black coffee.

"None of this surprised us after we'd been informed by more than one person that Amanda expressed her opinion the world would be better off without Eugene Geller. There were people who took her words seriously. We're also aware she and her sister Elena are very much at odds these days and have been for quite some time."

Malcolm stared out the window at a gloomy autumn day. "She's told us she doesn't regret that he's gone, though she claims not to have said she wished him dead. In fact, she denies ever saying that to anyone."

"So where was she on June twelfth?"

"She says on an extended shopping trip to Lexington. Though why she would drive down there to shop is beyond me, when we have great department stores right here in Cincinnati. We even have a store that features the kind of clothing and other items she might need on safari."

"She can't prove she was in Lexington, I take it."

"No receipts for purchases. She says she never keeps that kind of thing, and why would she ever dream she'd need to prove she'd been shopping in Lexington last June?"

"Well, she does have a point."

"Her daughter Autumn claims she was with her mother in Lexington, so there's that…but on the other hand, it's a family member. Never the best witness."

Augusta leaned back and observed Mal thoughtfully. "So, what's your next step?"

"Danny and Jim have some patrol people showing her photo around in Avondale to see if anyone remembers seeing her. Of course, at this point, that's probably an exercise in futility. We're talking four months ago, on a turbulent day. And of course we're re-interviewing all the people who were at Rockdale Temple that night, since the case has become a homicide."

He stood and went to the window, leaning against it as he stared outside. "One bit of progress in this case. Geller's car has been located, parked near an abandoned house out in Mt. Healthy. How it got there is a mystery, but the CPD had been keeping a lookout for it and we caught a break. The car has been towed to the crime lab to be examined."

Returning to the table, Mal drained his mug and refilled it. "Dolly Booth has been equally uncooperative. She denies her relationship with Geller was anything beyond friendship, and she claims to be devoted to her husband Leon. What's your understanding of her relationship with Geller, anyway? We've learned that the Booths and the Gellers have socialized on occasion. Does Leon Booth know of the rumor that two of his kids are actually Geller's offspring?"

"If he does, it appears he's chosen to ignore it. He absolutely adores Dolly and all six of the kids." Augusta finished her coffee. "I understand he's not living at home presently."

"That's correct, but Leon has been pretty much eliminated as a suspect. He was at a convention in Las Vegas which started on June twelfth, and he flew out there on the tenth. Three other people from his company were also on that trip. Leon didn't get home until the seventeenth."

"I honestly think you'll end up eliminating Dolly, and Elena, too, even though Elena's delay in reporting Gene missing is strange. And both women are in love with the man." Augusta shook her head. "But how Dolly can feel the same way about two men at the same time is beyond my comprehension."

Mal grinned. "While Gene feeling the same toward Elena and Dolly is something you get, right? A guy thing?"

"What's that jingle? 'Hogamous, Higamous, Men are polygamous; Higamous, Hogamous, Women monogamous'—or something like that."

"Where on earth did you hear that?" Mal laughed heartily. "Honestly, Gus, the stuff you come up with. But basically, I think there's truth to that. I'm with you, I can kind of understand Gene, but I do have a tough time with Dolly's—situation."

"You say she's being uncooperative. How so?"

"She's very…well, protective of Gene. Lots of tears for her wonderful friend the cantor. And she points fingers at both Elena and Amanda, saying either of them might have done away with him."

Augusta stood and collected the breakfast dishes. "So, you homicide detectives have a challenging case on your hands. My challenge is getting the opera workshop production on stage during this coming week. Larry should have the set ready for us for today's rehearsal. And I want to talk to him about the next project, *The Magic Flute.*"

Larry Rogers, a professional set designer with whom Augusta had a warm relationship, had been her set designer for Conservatory productions since she began directing.

Mal lifted an eyebrow. "Already? Isn't it a good idea to concentrate on one project at a time, even with Larry?"

"Oh, we'll just bat some ideas around while his crew is doing finishing touches." She wrapped her arms around Malcolm and kissed him. "And I'm sorry to say, I'll be late getting home…first full run is late this

80

afternoon. Martha offered to stop over and take care of Fritz."

Malcolm returned the kiss. "Isn't this one of Mrs. Bluefield's days to be here?" Henrietta Bluefield spent two days a week at the McKee-Mitchell home, sometimes more if needed.

"It is, but Martha wanted to bring Max over. You know how crazy your grandson is about Fritz. They'll have a good time taking him for a walk."

***

After completing her afternoon lessons, Augusta went to the Recital Hall to see how Larry was progressing with the set.

The production featured one act from each of two operas—both take place in a ballroom. Larry had created set pieces which were tall and scattered over the stage, and turning and respacing them created an entirely different ambiance. The *Hoffmann* sides of the set were covered in a metallic substance that provided changing reflections from the subtle colors in the stage lighting, giving a sense of dreaminess and unreality during the act. Turning the pieces for *La Cenerentola (Cinderella)* revealed bright, flowery, designs, creating a Rococo effect, an eighteenth-century look under brighter stage lights.

"Larry Rogers, once again you've demonstrated what a genius you are," Augusta commented admiringly as his staff put finishing touches on the pieces.

"This was a blast to design and create," Larry replied. "Just have your stage crew handle them gently. They're plenty stable but let's respect the paint, shall we?"

"Oh, absolutely. We'll take good care of them. Now, about *The Magic Flute*...." Augusta said.

Larry threw up his hands and laughed. "Give me a day or two to catch my breath, Madame Director. I'm studying the opera in my spare time, limited as it is."

"Then you know it's a fairy tale with a message."

"And of course, you'd like the set to reinforce that message."

"You know me so well," Augusta smiled.

"Let's get a coffee later this week before a rehearsal, and we can talk more about it."

"You're on."

Since she had about an hour before the cast began to arrive, Augusta took the time to continue thinking about what she would like to see on stage for the Mozart opera in the spring. *Good versus Evil, and confusion during part of the opera about who and what is good, and which characters represent evil. Prince Tamino is the lynchpin, in a way...we see most of this through his eyes. His and Pamina's. Lighting no doubt will be extremely important.*

How does this allegory of Mozart's relate to the situation in the world these days...or does it? I need to discuss all this with Dennis soon. Augusta smiled, thinking of her colleague, friend, and confidante, Father Dennis Halloran, a fellow faculty member at Cliffside College where she taught two days a week. They had known each other since his days as an undergraduate student at Xavier University, and the friendship only grew stronger after his ordination into the Society of Jesus and his return to teach at Xavier and Cliffside.

Augusta's cast and staff for the opera workshop production began to arrive in the auditorium, and she prepared herself for the task at hand.

***

The final week of rehearsals took most of Augusta's time, attention, and energy, and it was a relief not to have received any additional threatening. anonymous notes in the mail. She managed to push to the back of her mind the one she'd received.

Malcolm knew how much the show occupied her and for the most part steered clear of discussing the Eugene Geller murder case. He did let her know what the crime lab had turned up in its examination of Geller's car.

"Whoever drove the car to Mt. Healthy appears to have covered his tracks. They found blood in the trunk and are having that analyzed. I would bet my bottom dollar it's the same blood type as Geller's. The outside of the car is filthy; it's been sitting for months. Nearly a full tank of gas. There are fingerprints in the interior, but my bet is they'll be Geller's and the killer used gloves. Nothing appeared to be missing from the glove compartment, but of course we don't have Geller's wallet or driver's license."

"So you don't know much more than you did before you found the car."

"My theory is the murderer killed Geller, used his victim's car to dispose of the body, and then took the car to Mt. Healthy and left it there. He has to have Geller's wallet and car keys. But where the hell is this person? Better question: who the hell is this person?"

"I wish there were some way I could help."

"This is a tough one, for sure."

Malcolm gazed at Augusta, then shrugged. "I'm going to enjoy sitting through your show on Saturday night, and between now and then I will not mention the Geller case," he said as he kissed her. "You have enough on your mind."

Augusta was alert to the cast dynamics during the rest of the week, and she wasn't aware of any tension due to a more racially diverse cast. Final rehearsals went smoothly, and the first performance was received enthusiastically by the sold-out audience.

Backstage during intermission, she visited each dressing room and heard and saw the usual camaraderie among the cast members she had always witnessed during a production weekend. *All's well. Perhaps that note was an aberration after all*, she thought. She noticed George and Denise standing close to each other, holding hands. *More than a friendship, perhaps?*

Her stage director called out, "Ten minutes," and Augusta spoke briefly to George.

"Bocca al lupo, tenore." *In the mouth of the wolf, tenor.*

"Crepi," George responded with a grin. *May he die.*

Augusta made a point of speaking to the other principals—Angelica as Olympia, Allan Meissner as Coppelius, who seemed in his element to be on stage playing a villain, and the fourth principal in the act, mezzo-soprano Rachel Effron, playing the trouser role of Nicklausse, Hoffmann's companion. She then made her way to the back of the Recital Hall, where John Edmanston waited for her.

Seated next to John, it delighted Augusta when he turned to her at one point and quietly commented on Denise James' performance. "Even as an ensemble member, she's a standout, Augusta. Star quality, that one." It was nice to have her perception of Denise's talent and charisma confirmed by a colleague she respected and admired.

John's contribution to the evening, the second act of *La Cenerentola*, had been heartily applauded. Augusta's vision of *The Tales of Hoffmann's* first act concluded the evening, and Angelica, George, Allan, and Rachel all received prolonged ovations for their performances.

Augusta and John stayed at the back to "meet and greet" and thank audience members for supporting the Conservatory students. Watching the crowd disperse, Augusta saw no sign of any concerns or disapproval of her multi-ethnic cast, which included seven Black students and one each Chinese American and Japanese American student. *If anyone in this audience has a problem with my integrated cast, they're keeping it to themselves,* she thought.

Eloise Heinlein, one of the members of the Conservatory Board of Directors, stopped to speak with them. "Don't forget, party at my place tomorrow after the show," she gushed, pressing an envelope into each of their hands.

"Ta-ta." She waggled her fingers at them as she left. John and Augusta glanced at each other and had to cover their smiles. Eloise was hardly a favorite of either of them.

"We have to go," John said in a low voice. "But I'd rather listen to Harpo Marx sing."

Augusta covered her mouth and turned a laugh into a cough. "Harpo doesn't sing. He doesn't even talk."

"Exactly."

Chapter 8
A Party and a Duo of Ladies

Another sold-out house and strong audience reception for the workshop performance the following night. Mal made it to the show but had opted to pass on the party at Eloise Heinlein's, so Augusta persuaded Milly to be her date.

"I like most of the people on the Conservatory Board, but I just don't get Eloise," Milly commented on the drive to Indian Hill, the enclave of many of the wealthier denizens of Cincinnati. "Sorry, but she strikes me as pretentious and phony. What's with all that makeup, anyway? Didn't she ever hear the word 'subtle'?"

"Now tell us what you really think, Professor Devereaux," Augusta laughed.

"Well, honestly, Augusta. She has tons of money and a gorgeous house in Indian Hill, yet she seems to always be trying to find more ways to impress me when we talk."

Milly slowed for a traffic light. "She's had more trips to Europe. She's been on more cruises…well, she's got me there, I've never been on a cruise and never intend to go on one. I'm sure I'd be bored out of my skull. She buys her clothes in Europe. I've never had just a nice pleasant conversation with the woman about music. Shouldn't a member of the Board of the Conservatory think about music occasionally? Or am I being too logical?" She turned her head to stare at Augusta.

"Green light, Mil."

Milly returned her focus to her driving.

"Eloise inherited her spot on the board from her grandfather, if you recall," Augusta added. "What a dear he was. It is surprising she didn't seem to inherit any of the passion for music he had. Or his warmth or civility."

"Maybe she was a changeling child…switched at birth with the real Eloise Heinlein. It doesn't surprise me she's never married. No male could ever live up to her expectations. And I have absolutely no idea what those expectations might be."

Augusta laughed out loud. "Eloise is definitely one-of-a-kind, thank goodness. Let's make a pact. If she corners either one of us, the other is duty-bound to rescue the one she's entrapped."

The Heinlein manse sat in the center of at least fifteen acres of land, a neoclassical mansion that brought to mind Jefferson's Monticello. An attendant helped the women from Milly's car and parked it for them, another attendant at the door took their coats. Uniformed servers wandered through the crowd with offerings of beverages and hors d'oeuvres.

Augusta spotted John Edmanston and Byron Matthias and joined the group of board members they were chatting with, while Milly joined a former student and several piano teachers from the Conservatory in another group. They both continued to circulate and ended up in a clutch of board members with Eloise at the center.

Ignoring Milly and Augusta, Eloise chattered away about her mission of mercy, visiting an eccentric Cincinnati novelist serving a prison term in a state facility. Some two years earlier, Barry Whittier had killed two members of the Chrysanthemum String Quartet, one in Cincinnati and the other in Paris. The murder in Paris came to light during Augusta and Malcolm's honeymoon, and while Whittier had pleaded not guilty by reason of mental defect, he was found guilty and sentenced to prison for life. Eloise shared that dear Barry was undergoing extensive treatment and hoped he might have his case revisited.

"He's very sorry for what he did, now that he understands how wrong it was," Eloise announced.

This hit too close to home for Augusta because of her involvement in the case. She caught Milly's eye and the two managed to make their escape.

"Thanks for getting us out of there," Augusta said, once they were seated in Milly's car. "Barry Whittier. A name...and a time in my life...I do not like to revisit."

"Oh, I remember everything about that, and I understand perfectly. By the way, I heard some interesting gossip from one group I was with that you might pass on to Malcolm, though. Speculation about the Geller case."

"Oh?"

"Mostly what we'd already discussed—Amanda's intense dislike of her brother-in-law plus her local fame as a crack shot. Some talk about Leon Booth residing in the Cincinnati Club for the past few weeks. Do you think he might actually leave Dolly this time?"

"I highly doubt it. Was there any talk about how Gene Geller was killed? I think that information may have been given to the press recently, but not by the cops. Some enterprising reporter tracked down the surveyors who found the remains."

"I saw that article." Milly glanced toward her friend. "I'm sure whatever the surveyors told your buddy Arnie Richter at *The Morning Call*, the police would not confirm. If it's true his skull was bashed in, that pretty well eliminates Amanda. Now, if he'd been shot between the eyes, that would be another story."

"This isn't funny, Milly," Augusta chortled.

"Then why are you laughing? We hang out with the wrong kind of people, Augusta. Detectives and defense attorneys. We need to stop playing cops and robbers."

Augusta grew quiet. "It isn't funny at all. The homicide detectives are running into dead ends everywhere with this case. I know they've re-interviewed the staff at Rockdale Temple to attempt to reconstruct what happened on June twelfth. To learn if anyone saw Gene with someone at the Temple they didn't know, or if they saw anything that seemed suspicious as they got the kids out safely."

"Well, that would be difficult to spot in the middle of a riot, but I understand their need to track down any possible lead."

Augusta gazed at the oncoming headlights for a few moments. "Something else, and it doesn't have anything to do with the Geller case. I'm trying not to give this too much importance...but I got an anonymous note in the mail a few days ago."

"What kind of a note?"

"It warned me to be careful how I cast the opera."

Milly glanced at her friend. "You mean you were *threatened*? Why am I just hearing about this now?"

"I thought it was just a—oh, I don't even know, just something stupid someone sent. But I do wonder...do you suppose...could it possibly be one of the board members was responsible for sending it?"

Milly drove in silence for a time. "It's hard to imagine any of them would have sent it, even uppity Eloise. You haven't had any other threats, have you?"

"No, nothing. And I have to agree. Eloise would be the first person I'd suspect if I looked at the board. Dale tells me he's spoken with each of them privately and they are in agreement it's past time to give every student at the school the same opportunity. Eloise would probably know if she pulled something like that, she'd be the first person suspected. She may be a lot of things, but I've never had any reason to think she's stupid."

"Let's hope it was some snarky student who sent it on a whim. Maybe a soprano who's jealous of Denise, who seems to be a prime candidate for the role of

Pamina? You can't help but wonder where on earth it came from."

***

After a pleasant weekend with Malcolm, Augusta's week began peacefully enough with her routine of lessons, meetings, and continued preparations for auditions for *The Magic Flute*.

That changed abruptly just as she was clearing her desk and tidying her studio, ready to leave and head home. Loud female voices were heard in the hall. Without knocking, Elena Geller and Amanda Weatherly yanked open the door and stormed inside.

"You have to get your husband to make his detectives back off!" Amanda demanded. "I'm sick to death of being interrogated repeatedly about the same things. I've told them over and over that I was in Lexington on June twelfth, and my daughter Autumn has told them the same thing. And why are they involving my children in this, anyway? They wouldn't have had anything to do with their uncle's death."

"You don't know that for a fact," Elena sputtered. "All they ever heard from you was what a terrible person he was. Gene was a wonderful father, and you should know that, all my children told you that many times. After listening to all your trash talk, who knows what one of your children might have...."

"Don't you dare go there," Amanda warned, glaring at her sister. "Your husband abused you and I told you time and again to leave him."

92

"He never laid a finger on me," Elena screeched. "Never."

Augusta stared from one to the other, wondering how to remove this brawl from her peaceful studio. She closed the door and faced both of them. "I can't believe that you two…ladies…have come to the place where I practice my profession and simply burst in here to include me in a family feud. Both of you, sit down and…shut up."

Visibly stunned, both women obeyed.

"For all you knew, I could have been giving a lesson when you stormed in here." Augusta stood between them, glancing from one to the other. "If you have grievances with the Cincinnati Police Department, they won't be resolved in my private music studio. Whatever possessed you to come to me with these complaints, Amanda?"

"It's well known that you sometimes have worked on murder cases with Lieutenant Mitchell," Amanda huffed.

"You should know that this is not Lieutenant Mitchell's case. I made that clear to Elena. But since you're here…I can't believe how you're talking to your sister, who only recently learned that her husband was murdered. Have you even offered her your condolences and asked what you can do to be of help to her and your nieces and nephews during an incredibly difficult time?"

Amanda didn't respond, and Elena pulled a hankie from her purse and dabbed her eyes.

"Yes, Amanda, it would have been very nice to have heard some words of sympathy from you. I know you didn't like Gene, but he was my husband and the father of my children."

"I don't understand why…," Amanda grumbled, "…why the cops would think I could subdue a man physically who outweighed me by forty or fifty pounds and drag him off somewhere. And another thing, I don't like that the cops are questioning my friends."

"That's routine, Amanda. Since you realize you're a suspect, you should also realize the detectives will question your family and friends. Their sworn duty is to find whoever killed Eugene Geller and bring that person to justice."

Augusta crossed her arms over her chest as she spoke firmly to Amanda. "One last time…if you have complaints about the detectives who are handling Gene's murder, you need to take them to the police department. The crime of murder is considered a crime against the state," Augusta said. "Their sole responsibility is to find justice for the victim."

She turned to Elena. "And I'm a little surprised at you, coming here again, and bringing Amanda with you."

"She insisted," Elena almost whispered. "I apologize, Augusta. This whole situation has me so on edge. Gene's disappearance…and then learning he was murdered…and my poor, broken-hearted children." She lifted her hands as if in surrender.

Both women sat quietly for a moment.

Amanda glanced at Elena, who was dabbing at more tears now. Softening, she said, "I suppose I do need to apologize to you, Elena. You had nothing to do with the cops appearing at my door time and again. And I should have thought more about your children. I do love them, you know."

"And I adore Atticus and Autumn," Elena replied.

Augusta picked up her purse. "I was just leaving, and I need you to do the same. It seems to me the two of you need to go somewhere for coffee or a drink and have a good long talk."

The sisters stood, and Amanda impulsively grabbed Elena in a fierce hug. "She's right. Let's go to Meck's. I could do with a beer."

To Augusta's surprise but satisfaction, Elena returned the embrace, and the two sisters left her studio with their arms around each other, comparing notes on their children's reaction to Gene's death and completely ignoring Augusta.

Driving home, she ran through the conversation in her head and had to smile. *They must have driven their parents bonkers when they were growing up. Imagine those two as teenagers...never a dull moment in the Weatherly house.*

She recounted the entire adventure to Malcolm when he arrived home later that evening and they were relaxing in the living room after dinner. Fritz as always lay at Malcolm's feet, gazing up at him worshipfully.

"So things are okay between the Weatherly sisters now?" Mal asked.

"Well...when they left my studio, they seemed to be. But with that volatile a relationship, who knows how long their truce will last?"

She sipped her Drambuie. "They're both acting a little crazy if you ask me. Amanda of course has a point about the way Gene was so cavalier with his wedding vows. Elena has a point that he was a great father to his kids. Maybe they'll be able to work things out—providing neither of those women killed Gene."

"You'll be interested to know it appears Amanda has been telling the truth about her marathon shopping trip to Lexington." Mal took a swig of his beer. "She gave us a list of all the stores she visited, and one thing you have to say about Amanda, she's hard to forget. At least one clerk in every store remembered her vividly, and a search of their receipts for that date proved she'd spent a good bit of cash on the trip."

"What about the people in Avondale you were showing her picture to? Any luck with that?"

"Not to this point, and as we've said, Amanda isn't easy to forget."

"So she's no longer a suspect?" Augusta leaned back against the sofa.

"I wouldn't say that, but it does appear her alibi should hold up."

"Elena's alibi is solid, isn't it? She spent at least two weeks in Colorado with all four of her children."

"Again…it seems to be. The Boulder police are confirming with her cousins that she was with one or more of them the entire time."

"And you've said Leon Booth is definitely not a suspect."

"It seems not. His wife Dolly is vague about where she was, but with six children.…" Mal finished his beer.

"She's an interesting lady, but I think it would be tough to find time to kill somebody when you're dealing with six kids ages four to fourteen."

Augusta laughed. "Who's interviewed her? Danny and Jim both?"

Mal lifted an eyebrow. "If you can call it 'interviewing' when she's distracted every ten minutes by one child or another. Both of them have attempted to talk with her a couple of times. They tell me she's a sweet lady who seems a bit overwhelmed with taking care of six kids. It seems as if a lot doesn't get done in that house."

Augusta gazed at her aperitif glass. "So, your list of suspects is dwindling."

He nodded. "You remember I told you the lab found fingerprints inside the Geller car, and blood in the trunk. The blood is the same type as Geller's, O negative. Today we received his fingerprints from the Department of Defense, and the only identifiable prints in the car interior match those. So that doesn't help us at all. Another dead end."

Mal stared gloomily at Fritz, who laid his chin on his master's knee and whined softly. "Despite his philandering, Geller was well-liked—at the Temple and at his job. And at present, it appears the only woman other than his wife who he paid serious attention to was Dolly. There are rumors of other women. But we've found nothing specific."

"Gene's murder...it couldn't have been an accidental death during the riot, could it? I mean, since his body was moved and not found for months."

"It definitely appears he was targeted. Possibly by someone who for some reason knew he'd be at Rockdale Temple that day."

Mal rubbed Fritz's soft head. "So who the hell killed him?"

Chapter 9
Fairy Tales, and Life,
Can Be Complicated

Tuesdays and Thursdays were the two days Augusta taught at Cliffside College, and on the following Tuesday she made a point of staying on campus after she completed her lessons so she could have some time with Father Dennis Halloran. Dennis primarily had teaching and counseling duties at Xavier University. For the current semester, his scheduled classes at Cliffside coincided with Augusta's. They had made plans for Dennis to visit her studio, and he arrived bringing coffee and croissants he had picked up at a coffee house opposite the Alms Hotel in nearby Peebles Corner.

"Any word on the Eugene Geller murder case?" Dennis asked.

"Nothing new, I'm sorry to say." Augusta shook sugar into her coffee. "I hope the Black residents of Avondale aren't worried that the police think they're responsible for Gene's death. The entire city was on edge because of Laskey's conviction, and Gene did disappear the first night of the riot."

"I can understand why they might be concerned, but it seems to me that Eugene Geller's death was carefully plotted and planned, rather than his being a casualty of a night of racial rioting."

"About that," Augusta said, gazing at Dennis. "You understand why I want to present *The Magic Flute*, I'm sure. For one thing, I hope to defuse some of that ongoing tension."

"Yes, of course, you're looking at certain aspects of the plot that present a message…things aren't always what they seem. What appears to be evil can be good, and vice versa. There's always a reason to hope, and the truth will eventually be revealed. It's presented as a fairy tale, and it's somewhat confusing, but aren't most fairy tales?"

He buttered his croissant. "Tamino is a prince from who knows where, doing who knows what, and why is a serpent pursuing him? He's saved by Three Ladies who serve the Queen of the Night. He then meets a man who resembles a bird and acts like a birdbrain." Dennis arched an eyebrow, making Augusta laugh.

"Good description of Papageno. Go on."

Dennis continued his summary of the plot, speaking more and more rapidly. "Next Tamino sees a picture of Pamina, the Queen's daughter, and falls madly in love with her. The Queen shows up and sings a big coloratura aria, but not *the* aria. That comes later in the opera. Tamino is tasked with rescuing Pamina from Sarastro, but later we learn Sarastro had removed Pamina from her mother's care to save her."

Dennis abruptly paused and examined his croissant. "Here's a plot hole I've never understood—why would Sarastro, who is presented as all-wise and all-knowing, assign a lowlife like Monostatos to guard Pamina?"

Recovering from her laughter at his rapid-fire delivery, Augusta responded, "I always thought Sarastro placed Monostatos in that position because he was testing him. There was a spirit of some kind watching over Pamina, keeping her out of any real danger." Augusta broke off a piece of her croissant. "I know it's not in the script, but that was always my take on that element of the story."

"Interesting thought. I have a feeling in your production the audience may see that spirit…or maybe the Three Spirits, also characters in the opera, somewhere on stage during those scenes. That emphasis on threes…three ladies, three spirits, three tests for Tamino and Pamina. Like the three tenets of Freemasonry, which intrigued both Mozart and his librettist. Both were members of the organization, you know." Dennis took a healthy bite of croissant.

She nodded. "How do you feel about Mozart's use of symbolism from Freemasonry?"

"I think it's apparent Mozart's appreciation of the organization was more influenced by its emphasis on enlightenment and rationalism than on mysticism and the occult. It's my understanding that the overarching theme of Freemasonry is harmony. What could be more fitting for one of our greatest composers of all time? *The Magic*

Flute has a strong and hopeful message. That's what your audiences will come away with, despite the complicated plot."

Augusta smiled. "Yes, the plot is complicated, and it's kind of surprising it's a popular opera to present to children…though always shortened, with emphasis on the fairy tale elements. And some say the story boils down to growing up, finding your way in the world, and learning to love. Finding a way to distinguish what is true."

Thinking of what she hoped to put on stage brought a smile. "My production will definitely be fairy tale, Dennis. I want wonderful and fanciful costumes, with an unforgettable serpent at the beginning of the work. Beautiful and shocking."

"That all sounds ambitious, and I have no doubt you can make it happen." He drummed his fingers on the arm of his chair. "It also intrigues me that this is not an opera in the strictest sense—more like a musical theater piece, with spoken dialogue."

Augusta leaned forward. "Yes, *Singspiel*…maybe a forerunner of musical theater? Here's something important: I am hopeful some of the strong Black singers in our school will win featured roles in the opera. It's way past time that every voice student at the Conservatory had an equal opportunity for solo roles in any musical event. I can say without hesitation that race will not be a factor in how the show is cast."

Dennis took a swallow of coffee. "Well, more power to you, and I agree it's about time every vocal student had equal opportunity. But what about the instrumental students? How many Black students are in the Conservatory orchestra? Are any sitting first chair? Are any given the opportunity to conduct an ensemble?"

"Not as many as should be, I'm afraid," Augusta said. "I like to think that my world of music is ahead of society in being inclusive and makes all selections in whatever musical field based strictly on talent. Unfortunately, that's not always true."

"I'd have to agree. No major orchestra in this country has ever had a Black conductor. Nor in Europe, to the best of my knowledge."

"As far as that's concerned... there aren't any female orchestra conductors in the U.S., either, with the exception of Sarah Caldwell. She made her own opportunities when she established the Boston Opera Company, and acts as impresario, director, and conductor for that organization."

"Do you know the name Henry Lewis?" Dennis asked. "At sixteen, he broke the color barrier by performing as a bassist with the Los Angeles Philharmonic. Kind of the Jackie Robinson of classical orchestral music. Lewis has done some guest conducting and is brilliant. I think he'll have an opportunity to lead an orchestra soon. At least, I hope he will."

Augusta finished her coffee. "Back to my choice of Mozart's *The Magic Flute* for our spring production...I hope it may generate some feeling of goodwill. You know Mozart was very close to death when he wrote it, and I wonder if he had some premonition and wanted to leave a legacy with this work. It contains some of his best music."

"I would agree, though not everyone loves music from that era."

"That's true. I'm married to one who isn't a fan," Augusta chuckled, "though he loves many other operas."

"I assume you've chosen to perform it in English to make it more accessible to everyone, especially children." Dennis took a final bite of his croissant.

"Oh, absolutely. We'll be presenting a couple of shortened performances strictly for kids. They're the future and they need to see and hear something memorable. Something that may stay with them, and help them look at the world differently. I'm afraid what they've learned in school about racial injustice in the United States is limited."

Augusta finished her croissant and wiped her fingers on her napkin. "It's been a hundred years since the Civil War ended, Dennis. And change has been disastrously slow. If Lincoln had lived, we might be further along. But he didn't, and here we are, a nation still unwilling to provide many of our residents full citizenship. Or respect."

***

As she had explained to Milly about considering Denise James for the role of Pamina, Augusta had established rules for herself when hearing auditions and casting a production, whether at the Conservatory or at Cliffside. She gave her fellow directors first say as to their thoughts about the cast. It pleased her that to this point they had made the same choices she had in mind.

Looking over the lengthy cast list for *The Magic Flute*, Augusta calculated how many she could have in the ensemble. Some of the smaller roles, and even several speaking roles, could also be ensemble members. She thought a total cast of thirty to thirty-five onstage should work well.

Augusta had provided the same cast list to each member of the audition board, which consisted of herself; John Edmanston, who was acting as assistant director; Byron, her conductor; and Stacy, the choreographer. She also invited the rehearsal accompanist to give her input. Miriam was a senior piano major who would no doubt conduct some rehearsals. She had applied to Indiana University for graduate school in their conducting program and Augusta knew she aspired to directing opera in the future.

More than fifty students auditioned, among them quite a few freshmen who assumed they would most likely not be included in the cast but were encouraged to audition, if only for the experience. Some were Augusta's own students, and her advice to them was, "An audition is never wasted. You learn a lot about yourself, you've learned a new piece of music, and both of those fit nicely into your toolbox as an aspiring singer."

After solo auditions, the board asked to hear some voices together, especially from the women. "You know we want to hear a good balance and blend with the Three Ladies and the Three Spirits," John told them. "We want this cast to be all Conservatory students, so we are not considering using younger singers for the Spirits." This drew smiles from the women and they happily sang some sections of those trios.

"Since *The Magic Flute* also contains dialogue, we need to hear some readings," Augusta explained, as she passed out Xerox copies of sections of the show.

"Yes, this is unusual. And remember, all of you will have a dance audition with Stacy, also not a normal part of an opera audition. This is a fairy tale, and you're going to be moving differently than you ordinarily do in an opera. Think of this more as a stage musical with great music."

"Kind of like Gilbert and Sullivan?" asked Leroy Davis, John Edmanston's talented young Black baritone whom Augusta saw as a perfect Papageno.

"Yes, but with *much* more demanding music vocally," John replied.

The students reacted with laughter, chatting among themselves.

"Please look over the dialogue sections I just handed you, and if you're auditioning for a specific role, be sure you have a good idea who that character is."

For the next hour, the singers read short exchanges. Augusta was looking for the chemistry between two characters, such as Pamina and Tamino. Also between Papageno and Tamino, who are often on stage together.

Those auditioning had been advised to bring some kind of shoes appropriate for dancing—ballet slippers if they had them, or flexible, lightweight sneakers if not. Stacy saw eight students at a time on stage and taught them a routine that was minimally challenging but showed her what she needed to see. Some of the singers had obviously received dance training and were standouts, but there were others who picked up the routine quickly and also shone.

Following the dance audition, Augusta thanked the students for their interest in the production and told them the cast list would be posted on Friday.

Miriam alerted the cafeteria that the group in Recital Hall needed coffee and snacks, and they settled down to make decisions.

"Odd, that Mozart didn't give the lovers a duet," Stacy commented.

"Agreed. A trio for Pamina, Tamino and Sarastro. Pamina has a duet with Papageno but not Tamino. Papageno gets two duets, the one with her and the one with Papagena." A knock at the side door and Byron met the cafeteria server who rolled in a cart with coffee, sliced fruit, and cookies.

"One thing I'd like to request," Augusta said. "Papagena is easy to sing, but not so much to act. I'd like Stacy to weigh in on this one, since I think Papagena being able to move well could enhance the role and the duet with Papageno. And I think maybe in this instance, I'd like her to appear 'bird-like.' Maybe a small, slender girl."

She laughed. "Sounds like I'm casting a Broadway musical, doesn't it? Well, it's a very visual opera."

"Oh, good," Stacy responded with enthusiasm. "I'd hoped that would be a consideration." The board was in agreement, and settled down to discuss the principal roles.

"I'm ready to vote for our Tamino," John said. "George Van Dorn. I've never heard the aria performed better."

Three hands went up in agreement. "He's got a future ahead of him," Byron commented.

"I'm quite happy with your choice," Augusta said. "As his teacher, I have to add that George has become a model student and is very focused on a career."

"I'm glad you asked him to read with Denise James," Byron said. "Because I can see that being the perfect match for him as Pamina."

John, Stacy, and Miriam added their agreement on this role.

"Are you sure?" Augusta asked. "It always gives me pause when I'm casting two of my own students in leading roles."

"It's happened before," Byron commented. "As always, Augusta, we're not offering them these roles because they're your students, and you know that. They are both right for the roles, and we all saw the chemistry between them."

Another easy decision was Leroy Davis as Papageno. "The kid just sparkles," Stacy said. "And he moves so well…I'm sure he's had some dance training. I can have so much fun with him."

"Also, I liked his reading with George," Augusta remarked. "They really clicked."

The Queen of the Night was an easy decision, as was Sarastro. Angelica Costa was the only coloratura who could securely handle the "Vengeance Aria," the most important element of that role. And Allan Meissner, with his deep, rich basso and imposing height, was a given for Sarastro.

Stacy asked if she could have a few sopranos back for a special dance audition for Papagena, and all were in agreement. The board quickly filled out the remainder of the cast list, only debating the Three Ladies and Three Spirits...they liked the same six singers but saw them in different configurations. Augusta suggested it should be Byron's call. "He's going to be working most closely with them."

On Augusta's drive home she felt well satisfied. *This is going to be an excellent production. I liked the feeling in the room during the auditions, it's apparent the cast is excited about being part of Mozart's fairy tale.*

She entered her home to be greeted by Fritz and saw Malcolm had brought in the mail. He wandered into the entrance hall and gave her a warm embrace.

"You look pleased, so I'm going to guess you managed to get your show cast."

"We did. An excellent cast, I'm happy to say. And as a bonus, two deserving Black students in leading roles."

She shuffled through the mail, pausing when she found an envelope stuck inside a magazine. Augusta felt a flutter in her chest as she held it up to show Malcolm. It was identical to the one she had received some two weeks earlier. No return address, and her address printed in block capitals.

He took it from her, handling it carefully as he opened it.

"Another threat?" Augusta's voice shook slightly as she sat down abruptly.

"Sorry to say, yes," he replied, showing her the note.

ACCIDENTS CAN HAPPEN AT ANY TIME

Chapter 10
Serpents Come in Different Shapes

"I don't like this at all, Gus." Mal frowned as he carefully put the note back in the envelope. "One 'hate message' is a matter of concern. Two could mean someone is clearly threatening you."

"These notes are unsettling, I'll admit." Augusta crossed her arms over her chest. "But I don't understand at all why I've received this one on the very day I've just made casting decisions. We won't post the cast list until Friday, so where is this coming from? I hate to think this, but I have to wonder if it could be some student who wants a leading role and is resorting to this kind of nonsense to sway my decision." She reached down to pat Fritz's flanks.

Mal lifted an eyebrow. "I still don't like it. There was always the possibility you could cast a Black soprano opposite a white tenor in a town that's still jumpy with racial tension. This could be a legitimate threat."

"Well, that's exactly how the casting worked out— Denise James and George Van Dorn. The two singers who were the strongest contenders for those roles. That was our only consideration. The students are pretty savvy, and I'm sure they were aware the casting could go that way whether they liked it or not. But again, the list won't be posted for a couple more days."

She turned to go into the kitchen. "Honestly, Mal, I hate all of this…this racial division in our country. I know it exists, and I know somehow it has to be dealt with. But I can't deal with it right now."

She opened the refrigerator door. "There's leftover lasagna, does that sound okay?"

Malcolm followed her and the two worked companionably as they prepared their meal.

"Word travels fast in Cincinnati, Gus. It's basically a big small town, you're well aware of that." He paused after setting plates on the table in the alcove. "I'm sure you had 'locals' who auditioned for this production. Your stalker could be a relative or friend of one of those."

"Yes, there were some resident Cincinnatians in our audition pool. Some were excellent. And of course, both George and Denise are locals." Augusta slipped Fritz a small piece of cheese which he swallowed without even blinking.

"Gus, I really think it's a bad idea to hand-feed him." Malcolm opened the refrigerator. "Do you want salad? Or something else?"

"I'll make a quick Mediterranean fruit salad. There are bananas, pears, and grapes…I can put those together while the lasagna is heating."

"Nice to hear George will be performing a lead. Good for him." Mal pointed to a corner. "Fritz, sit." Fritz gazed at him reproachfully but obeyed, slinking into the corner and curling up.

As they settled into their chairs, food on plates, Augusta picked up the conversation again. "I hope you are not going to suggest a protective detail for me. Please don't do that. The CPD doesn't have the manpower, for one thing. They need to be able to quickly commandeer as many cops as possible in case of some kind of flareup. And anyway, I'm quite capable of taking care of myself."

"Would you care to elaborate on that last comment?"

"I can change my routine slightly, leaving the house a little earlier, or later. I can vary the routes I drive to the Conservatory and Cliffside and stay vigilant about the cars around me. If I leave after dark I'll have a student, or maybe the night watchman, walk me to my car. I've learned a lot in the four years we've been together, Lieutenant Mitchell."

She took a forkful of lasagna. "All the routes I drive are well traveled and I often see patrol cars. If necessary, I could flag one down. And one other thing…I think I need to do daily practice at the Revolver Club."

Augusta didn't say it, but she was sure Malcolm understood that would mean she'd have her gun with her. And she was also sure he knew she would use it if necessary.

"I still don't like this," Mal said. "But two rather vague notes don't justify me assigning a protective detail at this point. However, I will talk to Danny and Jim.

Don't be too dismissive of hate mail, Gus. Things are different these days."

"I'm very much aware of that." She sighed. "Do you remember that entertaining quote from Mark Twain about our city?"

Mal gave her a lopsided grin. "He supposedly said something about wanting to be in Cincinnati when the world comes to an end because we're always twenty years behind the times." They chuckled, and Mal grew serious. "A lot has changed since the riot in June and the crime spree that led up to it, sad to say."

"One of the things I hate most about this climate we're living in is that some people seem to have forgotten what a great police force we have here, in many ways thanks to how forward-thinking Stan Schrotel was," Augusta remarked.

"You mean how he integrated the force, I'm sure. Along with being an exemplary member of law enforcement, the Chief had an unequaled sense of fairness. I know you've mentioned recently how important you think it is for performers in the music world to be considered strictly by their ability…which is what you're doing with your casting for this opera. The Chief felt the same about every person on the CPD."

"Yes, something he was much admired for." Augusta took a small bite of lasagna.

"Did I ever tell you about how that integration in the force began? As with most police departments in this country, Black officers policed Black neighborhoods, with white officers assigned to white neighborhoods.

Yes, I know. Segregation. But it was the norm for decades."

"Yes, it certainly was. So, what happened to effect the change?"

Mal pushed his chair back. "Well, I think it was about ten years ago when Policewoman Lillian Grigsby caught three white truants from Northern Kentucky in downtown Cincinnati on a school day. The father of one claimed to be a 'friend' of the Chief and called him to complain that a Black policewoman arrested his son. Schrotel called him to his office to resolve the issue, and also 'invited' Grigsby. She was sure she was about to be fired because most people invited to his office under those circumstances were."

"I suspect that didn't happen that day, though."

"When the three of them were in his office, Schrotel said to the truant's father, 'This is Cincinnati Policewoman Grigsby. She is a police officer in the Cincinnati Police Division just like every other police officer in my department. If you don't want your son arrested by her when he decides to cut school, keep him on your side of the Ohio River.' After that incident, the Chief decided that he needed to have some Black officers in white neighborhoods and vice versa, and eventually also began integrating patrol cars. You know Danny's former partner, Jesse Wilkins."

"Terrific young guy. They've remained close friends, even though Dan is now in Homicide."

Mal finished his lasagna. "It's true the tension in this city makes our work more difficult, but we still do it."

"And you still love it." Augusta laid her hand on his wrist. "Mal, I know how frustrating it is to keep running into dead ends with the Geller case. But I also know your detectives will uncover the puzzle pieces they need, and find the killer."

***

Before leaving her house, Augusta glanced at the calendar. *Friday, October 27. November is only days away*, she mused, *and Gene Geller's killer is still out there somewhere.*

She turned up the heat slightly in her 1963 sapphire blue Chrysler Imperial. Overnight, the weather had changed, and the pleasant fall they had been enjoying would become winter sooner than people liked. *Well, this is the way it often happens,* Augusta thought, shivering slightly as the car warmed.

Remembering her plan to vary her travel to and from the Conservatory or Cliffside, Augusta turned left rather than right onto Madison Road, and worked her way through Hyde Park to Edwards Road and eventually to Columbia Parkway, where she headed for Eden Park. She'd given herself an extra hour, and on this brisk, bright, late autumn day, she enjoyed the drive through a favorite part of her city.

Only days earlier the park had been a riot of color. Now leaves were falling fast, especially in the stiff wind. Whatever the season, Augusta loved her city's urban park. No matter how far she traveled, she still felt she would put this beautiful hill up against anything she'd seen anywhere else. She also loved driving her Chrysler. Even though it was now over four years old, she was reluctant to trade it for a newer model. She kept it in top shape and felt it should be good for at least another year.

Finally, she parked near the Conservatory and walked up the winding drive to Main Hall, through the ornate Victorian entryway, and up the curved staircase to Milly's studio. They had a nine-thirty meeting to finalize their program for Sunday afternoon. They were taking several voice and piano students to entertain residents of the River View Care Center, a retirement home in Northern Kentucky. A former organ teacher at the Conservatory, Titus Powlett, had been one of those residents for some time, and once Augusta and Milly learned of that, they made a point of visiting him several times a year.

Milly stood in the doorway watching her friend approach. "You're early."

"Not by much. I took the long way around today, coming through Eden Park. We do live in a beautiful city."

Milly waited until Augusta was seated and handed her a sheet of paper. "The office did these programs for us for the retirement home, and I asked for this large print."

Augusta examined it. "It looks beautiful. Thanks for taking care of that."

"All of the student performers are set for Sunday, I believe. Including your two—'Tamino' and 'Pamina'?"

Augusta smiled. "The cast list for *The Magic Flute* goes up at the end of the day today, and yes, George and

Denise will be performing those roles. You predicted correctly."

Milly studied the program. "I love this duet you asked them to sing at the retirement home. The one from the 'Antonia act' of *The Tales of Hoffmann*. Oh, and I talked to Titus last night. He's thrilled we're coming."

"He does seem to enjoy our musicales. I hope his fellow residents are as appreciative as he is."

"I doubt they are as attuned to how well these students perform, but they seem to like it," Milly laughed. "Most of them, anyway."

"How about transportation? Are we good with that?" Augusta folded the program she'd been perusing.

"Yes, rather than have the students drive, we've borrowed a bus from Walnut Hills High School. They were very obliging."

"Thanks for handling all this, Mil," Augusta said.

"Well, you've had your hands full, first with the opera workshop performances and then with auditions for the spring opera. I was happy to do it."

Augusta stood, preparing to go downstairs to her studio, but Milly stopped her.

"I don't know if you'd heard this. I suppose Mal may have. Dolly Booth has filed for divorce."

Augusta stared at her and sat down to process this. "*What*? That's hard to believe, even though her husband hasn't been living at home for several weeks. She's divorcing Leon? On what grounds?"

"Garrett gave me that information last night. Incompatibility is what he was told."

"After six children, of which at least four are unquestionably Leon's? That seems a stretch, don't you think?" She gazed at Milly. "Maybe the stress of being questioned about Gene's murder prompted the breakup. It's possible Leon is being generous and allowing Dolly to file."

"I have no idea why this happened," Milly replied. "I didn't think you'd heard, though. I'm sure the homicide detectives know by now."

"Well, an interesting start to my day. And an interesting end as well...I'm posting the cast list for *The Magic Flute* at four o'clock, and then getting the heck out of here."

"Sounds like a good plan. I'll pick you up Sunday. About noon? I want to get to River View before the students arrive at one-thirty."

Augusta hesitated. "We need to talk about that. I might as well tell you...I had another anonymous letter. Mal is concerned."

"Another note? What did it say?"

"It said 'accidents can happen at any time,' or something like that." Augusta waved a hand. "But honestly, I don't know that it's anything to worry about."

"That certainly sounds like a threat to me. I'm not surprised Mal is concerned about this. Does he know about our plans for Sunday?"

"Yes, I told him. He suggested it might not be a bad idea for him to drive us across the river, but I told him I didn't think that was necessary."

"I would really hate to cancel this program, which would be another option," Milly said.

"We're not doing that." Augusta stood again and turned toward the door. "But don't be too surprised if we end up with an escort courtesy of the CPD."

Augusta's mail when she reached home that afternoon confirmed her prophecy that she and Milly would have that escort. Another anonymous envelope, exactly like the first two. Her hand shook slightly as she opened it.

START SAYING YOUR PRAYERS

Chapter 11
An Afternoon of Music

Sunday, October 29

Milly turned onto the John Roebling Suspension Bridge and watched the car behind her stay just far enough back so it wasn't obvious Danny and Jim were keeping her under observation.

"Well, this is a first. I've never been escorted to a performance by a couple of detectives before," Milly remarked.

"Mal and Danny talked, and Danny offered to make sure we got here safely. I have to admit, that third message made me very uneasy." Augusta sighed. "Mal said three anonymous notes still didn't prove anything, and he couldn't justify providing us an official escort. Danny is sweet to be so protective, and I have to say I'm glad they're with us. But I guess part of me hopes this is all about some unhappy soprano who wanted the role of Pamina."

"But who? You said you didn't see any hostility during auditions."

"I didn't. And I haven't any idea who it might be. I just hope we didn't cast whoever it was at all so there won't be any unpleasantness during rehearsals."

Augusta watched the city of Covington spread out at the other end of the bridge. As often as she had made this drive, she always found it enjoyable, appreciating John Roebling's edifice as a true work of art. At the time it opened a hundred years earlier, it was the longest suspension bridge in the world. The Roebling Bridge had considerably eased the steamboat traffic that swarmed between Cincinnati and the Northern Kentucky towns on the opposite shore.

Milly exited the bridge and headed southwest toward the charming town of Florence and the River View Care Center. "I'm not sure why they named this facility 'River View' since the Ohio isn't anywhere in sight."

"Yes, but it's a nice name, and maybe from the rooftop you can glimpse the river on a clear day," Augusta laughed.

Even though it was a pleasant, sunny day, they were surprised and touched to see Titus Powlett waiting outside when they arrived. It caused Augusta's stomach to clench slightly to see him in a wheelchair rather than using a walker. *Well, he is over ninety. None of us lives forever, but he's such a treasure. He'll be sorely missed when he's gone.*

Titus quickly wheeled the chair toward them with a flourish, as if he were driving a race car. "Ah, my two favorite ladies." He beamed at them.

Augusta and Milly each kissed his cheek and he motioned them to follow him into the reception hall.

"I think we've set this up so it will work for the program." He waved toward one end of the room where the piano was set in the center at an angle, and chairs for the audience had been arranged in rows.

"It's perfect," Milly told him, heading for the piano. She sat and played chords and arpeggios. "Oh, you just had the piano tuned, too."

"Did you expect anything less?" Titus chuckled. "When are your performers arriving?"

"They should be here by one-thirty. Augusta will do a group warm-up with the singers and we can start right at two as we planned," Milly said.

Titus wheeled his chair closer to the piano. "I can't tell you how much I appreciate your doing this. We all do. Some of the residents may not really hear much...," he winked at them, "...and some may not be big fans of classical music, but it's still a festive occasion even for them."

Milly handed one of the programs to Titus. "Not strictly classical today. Some musical theater pieces, and I have one of my students playing the themes from Gershwin's 'Rhapsody in Blue.' What's not to like about that?"

Titus studied the program and glanced up at Milly, his eyes twinkling. "This strikes me as pretty much perfect. Looks like about an hour and a half, just the right length. Every member of your audience may manage to stay awake."

The three of them laughed. "And as promised, our gang is bringing desserts from the Conservatory kitchen…the cooks wanted to contribute to the festivities," Augusta said.

Titus motioned toward a side wall where a long table was set up draped in tablecloths and holding a punch bowl and coffee maker. "This musical party is such a nice treat for us."

"And for us," Milly said.

The performers were ushered in and attendants of the facility received the baked goods and placed them on the tables. Augusta introduced the students to "my dear friend, Dr. Titus Powlett, formerly a great organ teacher at the Conservatory." Titus greeted all twelve of them and impressed the entire group by remembering each of their names as he charmed them all with his questions and amicable chatter.

The other residents began to arrive, some using walkers, some in wheelchairs, and some being assisted by attendants. Titus had suggested the students circulate and introduce themselves, which they did. Augusta believed from their facial expressions they were thinking of elderly relatives and were happy to have this opportunity to bring some music and light into the lives of the residents.

Augusta noticed that George and Denise were often together. *Well, that's interesting. Of course, they were just cast opposite each other in the opera. But it seems this might be something more.*

Titus began the program by introducing Milly and Augusta and thanking them for bringing a program to the

River View. Augusta had included selections by Cole Porter, Jerome Kern, and Rodgers and Hammerstein, along with selections performed in English from lighter operas: *The Marriage of Figaro* and *The Bartered Bride*. George and Denise's lovely duet from *The Tales of Hoffmann* received prolonged applause.

Piano selections included well-known pieces such as Debussy's "Clair de lune" and Chopin's "Raindrop Prelude," as well as Rachmaninoff's much-loved Prelude in C-Sharp Minor.

Milly told an entertaining story about that piece. "Rachmaninoff was always expected to play it at least as an encore when he gave one of his numerous recitals and he began to tire of playing it. He'd written it when he was nineteen and still a music student. Near the end of his life, he absolutely refused to play it and would indicate to the audience they were *not* going to hear that Prelude, no matter what. He would firmly close the cover over the keyboard and leave the stage."

She added, "I can understand why. It was one of the first pieces he ever wrote, and he thought his later works had much more merit and deserved to be heard more than the C-sharp minor prelude. But people still loved it...and we're thrilled to share it with you today."

Those in the audience who were able gave the performers a standing ovation at the end of the program, and then audience and performers mingled as they enjoyed refreshments. Milly and Augusta took advantage of this time to move with Titus to a small table in a corner where they could talk.

"So, Augusta, is Lieutenant Mitchell making headway with his investigation of Gene Geller's murder? Such a shock to learn of the discovery of his remains all those months after he disappeared." Titus tasted a slice of cherry pie.

"Not much," Augusta responded. "It's frustrating. But the homicide division is doing everything they can, trying to find leads."

"Did you know Eugene Geller?" Milly asked.

"Oh, I did indeed. You know, he was not a music major. He was majoring in business administration at the University, but he minored in music. So he was on the Conservatory campus I think two days a week. I didn't see much of him since he wasn't a keyboard student, but even then, he was doing some cantorial work at Rockdale Temple, and I sometimes substituted for their organist."

"What do you remember about him during his college days?" Augusta asked.

"He was a charming young man. A bit of a rascal, but very likable. He had an unusually beautiful baritone voice even as a young college student. And he had that special gift of innate musicality and was always a pleasure to hear." Titus took another bite and chewed thoughtfully for a few minutes. "Gene was easy to like. Some people have that gift, and it's mainly because they genuinely are open and friendly. That was his charm. He was curious about everyone he met and people opened up to him."

"Women more than men?" Milly asked.

"Certainly women, but men, too. People liked being around him." He paused for a moment. "Except one

126

person that I recall. Elena used to come to the Conservatory with Gene sometimes. It was evident they were enamored with each other from the time they were sophomores, and it looked like they might be headed for marriage."

He wiped his mouth. "Please thank those nice cooks for these goodies, will you? I don't remember having pie this good when I was at the Conservatory."

"I'll pass on your compliments," Milly laughed. "You were saying something about one person who wasn't charmed by Gene."

Titus nodded. "Elena was a lovely young woman. There was another student at the University of Cincinnati who was quite smitten with her."

"Another love triangle, Titus?" asked Augusta. "You were a great help to Mal when the long-ago murder of Wesley Vandergriff was discovered fairly recently. What you recalled about that very sad situation was invaluable in solving the case."

"Well, of course, that had all happened decades earlier. And I knew Wesley much better than I knew Eugene, since Wes was my student and later became a good friend."

He gazed into the distance. "The situation with Gene and his would-be rival for Elena wasn't nearly as intense as Wesley's romance with sweet Alice, who loved Wesley but married her other suitor, Thomas Reichenbach, at her father's insistence."

"Yes, and as you said, that was another era," Augusta commented.

Titus nodded. "In any event, Elena did nothing to encourage her would-be beau, but he pursued her however and whenever he could. Sometimes he just showed up at the Conservatory, even though he wasn't taking lessons or enrolled in any classes. He was there because Elena was there. I think that caused some problems for a time between Elena and Gene."

"In what way?" Milly sipped her coffee.

"Mainly just that the young man was extremely persistent. Poor Elena avoided him as much as she could, but he made a point of hanging around her whenever possible. Gene confronted him in the entrance to Main Hall one day and told him in no uncertain terms to leave Elena alone, that they were practically engaged. It was one of the few times—maybe the only time—I ever saw Gene angry."

"So, the young man was probably jealous of Gene," Augusta said.

"Without a doubt. Gene had the woman he had his eye on, and Gene was a singer, which appealed to Elena. I believe her unwanted suitor dropped out of U.C. after the first semester of their junior year…if I recall correctly."

"Do you know what happened to him?" Milly said.

"No, never heard anything about him after he left. Oh, one thing I do remember, he was from the south. Alabama, I think. It could be he went to school down there after leaving Cincinnati. I don't believe I ever saw him again."

One of the attendants came by with the cherry pie and served Titus another slice.

"Love triangles…they seem to happen a lot," he chuckled. "Anyway, all the recent publicity about Gene reminded me of this one."

"What was Gene's rival's name?" asked Augusta.

"Benjamin…Richards? Roberts? It'll come to me."

Augusta stood and saw that residents were being taken back to their rooms. It pleased her to see some students hugging their new friends. *Good, they've learned how vital music can be to everyone, how important it is to bring beauty into the lives of many diverse groups…and maybe especially the very old.*

Since the Conservatory kitchen had provided disposable packaging there was no need to collect anything, and the students began to don their coats.

Titus moved with Augusta and Milly toward the group of Conservatory students.

"I can't thank you enough for coming to visit us and bringing us wonderful music, performed beautifully," he said to them. "You can't begin to know how much it means to old folks like us to be made to feel special by special people."

"You're the ones who are special, Professor Powlett," George said. "It was a privilege for us to spend the afternoon with you."

The students gathered around Titus, shaking his hand, some of the girls embracing him. Denise impulsively kissed his cheek and he chuckled. "Thank you, young lady. You know how to make an old geezer feel young for a moment."

The bus driver had remained to enjoy the program, and now motioned to the students to return to the bus.

"Let's go, folks. I promised I'd have you back to the Conservatory by five at the latest."

After they left, Milly and Augusta lingered for a few more moments, reluctant to leave Titus. "Call us whenever you'd like to talk," Milly told him. "About anything."

"I just may do that, Milly…Augusta." One last hug and they departed.

Augusta was quiet on the drive back to Cincinnati.

"Penny for your thoughts."

"I'm just trying to imagine what it would be like…Milly, he's remarkable, and he's approaching his mid-nineties. I think he's been at River View for seven years. He chose to become a resident there when he simply wasn't able to continue living alone."

"It was sad when he realized his back problems meant he could no longer play the organ. But you and I know he plays the piano there at River View daily. If and when I ever grow up, I want to be just like Titus Powlett," Milly vowed as she turned onto the entrance ramp to the bridge.

"What Titus told us about Gene Geller being irresistible," Milly said. "I was quite intrigued by him. I met him at a party not long after I came back from California, and I was totally charmed. Fortunately, I kept my wits about me."

"You mean he made a pass at you?" Augusta stared at her

"I don't think the man could help himself. He just loved women…even older women."

"Why am I only hearing this now?"

"I didn't take it seriously, and frankly, only remembered it today because of Titus' story. Now, there is a man who is really something. I'm glad he's still around to regale us with his stories."

"He's an inspiration," Augusta said. "I'm so glad he continues to be part of our lives. We'll come back at Christmas."

Milly glanced at her friend. "By the way, Augusta…."

"Yes, Mil, I'm thinking the same thing. I love you, too. I can't imagine not having you as my best friend. We're very lucky to have each other."

Chapter 12
Sometimes Things Are Not What They Seem

After escorting Milly home, Danny and Jim drove Augusta to the Mitchell house, where they stayed for a few minutes to talk to Malcolm. Fritz greeted all of them when they entered the house, and Danny found treats to give his baby boy's buddy.

"How'd it go?" Mal kissed Augusta briefly.

"It was truly lovely," she replied.

As often happened, when their eyes met a look passed between them, something Augusta had come to cherish. She hoped there would always be that special glance, an unspoken reminder of the strength of their connection.

"I'll leave you gentlemen alone since I know you want to discuss the Geller case." She prepared to go upstairs.

"No, stay," Mal said. "This is an informal conversation, and you might have something to contribute."

Seated in the alcove, coffee on the table, Jim explained, "Dolly Booth filing for divorce so abruptly has prompted us to re-investigate Leon's trip to Vegas." He glanced around the table. "One thing we've learned which needs to be examined more thoroughly is that Booth had a private room at the resort where the convention was held."

"Which means there was not always someone else with him during the time they were there," Mal mused.

"Right. We need to find out more about that convention," Danny took a swallow of coffee. "Generally, for an event like that, there are sometimes multiple sessions taking place at the same time, and it's unlikely the attendees knew exactly where the others were the whole time."

"Don't you think they might have had someone in charge keeping track of each person's itinerary, though?" Augusta asked.

"That could be. On the other hand, it's entirely possible even if they had indicated which sessions they wanted to attend, they might have changed their plans once they actually got to the convention," Jim commented.

"So Booth might have been able to slip away during the convention without anyone noticing," Mal said. "It's hard to believe, though, that he could have been missing for two days without anyone realizing it. And if he'd made a trip back to Cincinnati, he would have probably needed that time to fly both ways."

"On the other hand, if he did that, I doubt he would have flown commercially," Jim said. "More likely hired a private plane. We checked the flight time, and it's about four hours. So he could have made such a trip and had time to do whatever else he planned within a twenty-four hour period."

Augusta stared around the table. "It's hard to imagine Leon planning to kill anybody, even if he had a good reason. Hiring a private plane…that would be incredibly expensive, wouldn't it?"

"Yes, and if that happened, he probably would have used a different name. But I think Dan and Jim are right, it does need to be considered." Malcolm brought the coffee carafe to the table and refilled the men's cups, while Augusta covered hers with a hand and shook her head no.

"So we think we need to re-interview every person who was on that trip and find out when they actually spent time with Booth," Jim concluded.

"At the moment, it appears worth investigating," Malcolm told them. "Probably a long shot, but you never know what you might find when you start digging."

Augusta checked her watch. "Mal, Ryan and Lacey should be here shortly."

"And I have to get home to collect my family," Danny grinned. Lacey and Martha had wanted to have a family dinner at Mal and Augusta's that Sunday, and had offered to do all the cooking since they knew how busy Augusta was that weekend.

After Danny and Jim left, Mal fed and walked Fritz while Augusta cleaned the kitchen and put away the coffee mugs before setting the table. Looking through the window at the quiet beauty of autumnal daylight on her now dormant garden, she thought again of the gaze she and Mal had shared earlier.

The first time they'd shared such a moment was under the direst circumstances imaginable. Augusta had a criminal's arm around her shoulders from behind and a gun held to her head. Mal knelt on the floor in front of them, gazing into her eyes. When the man holding her was momentarily distracted, Mal and Augusta acted in unison: she driving her stiletto heel into his ankle as Mal leapt up and knocked his hand above his head. The gun discharged into the door frame as the goon fell to the floor, clutching his ankle.

That was the second time Mal had saved her life since she'd become involved in cases he was working. After a rocky start to their relationship, they had gone on to work well together to resolve several murder cases— Augusta in an unofficial capacity, of course. Mal had come to appreciate her good instincts. *Despite my occasional overstepping, which Mal definitely didn't like if that overstepping put my life in danger,* she mused.

And now, here was another difficult case. Could Leon Booth have actually found some way to do away with his rival? Leon appeared to be a quiet, upright man, seemingly accepting his wife's infidelity. But perhaps he had not.

Evil can appear as good, she thought. *A theme in Mozart's opera, represented primarily by the Queen of the Night. She presents herself as wronged by "the evil Sarastro." We don't really see her as otherwise until she shows her true colors in her "Vengeance Aria."*

***

A delicious dinner devoured and the extra food put into containers and in the refrigerator, the Mitchell family took some time to relax in the living room. The focus was on little Max, happily seated on blankets spread over the carpet. Fritz lay nearby, ears perked up, a vigilant guard.

"He'll be crawling soon," Malcolm said, from his spot on the living room floor near the baby. "Be ready, Martha. It's amazing how fast they can move once they figure it out."

Max threw his favorite rattle at his grandfather, who caught it deftly and returned it...only to see it come right back at him.

"That's his favorite game, Dad," Danny laughed. "By the way...have you thought yet about what you'd like him to call you? Probably not Gramps." Laughter all around.

"How about Granddaddy? That works for me," Mal replied.

Martha exchanged a glance with Ryan's wife Lacey. The women were the only ones seated on furniture, all three men were on the floor with Max and Fritz. Warm oriental carpeting in soft shades of green, gold, cerulean blue, and cream covered much of the floor, echoing the colors in the comfortable stuffed furniture.

Augusta noticed the glance exchanged between the two women. "I believe I know what you're thinking," she announced.

"Well…no way can I see you as 'Grandma,'" Lacey said. "And Carla has claimed 'Grandmommy.'" Augusta caught the inflection which confirmed that Mal's ex-wife was not a favorite of either of his daughters-in-law. Both Lacey and Martha were immensely fond of Augusta…Martha in particular, who still took occasional lessons from the teacher she adored.

"Of course, she has," Augusta said. "Not to worry. I've actually been thinking about this, believe it or not. How about Grandmere? I like all things French."

Max tossed the rattle again and his father caught it this time and shook it as the baby gurgled and guffawed, reaching out to retrieve it. Danny briefly teased him with it before handing it to his son.

"I love it," Martha said. "I think it suits you perfectly. And Dad, would you rather be 'Grandpere'?"

"Oh, I'm not sure I have enough experience in France to qualify," Mal winked at Augusta. "You have to remember, Augusta lived in Europe for three years after she graduated from the Conservatory, and spent most of that time in Paris."

The two young women went into the kitchen to finish cleaning up, and Danny and Ryan took Max and Fritz for a quick walk as the sun was setting. Mal and Augusta collected toys and blankets from the floor.

"So, you like all things French, Augusta," Mal commented, a grin tugging at his lips.

"Oh, shush. I wasn't even thinking about Jean-Luc. That was so long ago it's become the faintest of memories…and would be gone completely if you didn't take every opportunity to tease me about it." She shook out a blanket and folded it, stacking it on the sofa.

"Sorry, bride. I just can't resist."

"And I'm sorry you met him when we were in Paris on our honeymoon. I still can't believe you invited him to have drinks with us when you were pretty sure he was the same man I'd been involved with decades ago."

"I didn't know that for a fact." Malcolm reached for her but Augusta shook him off. "How else was I to confirm it?"

"Well, you chose to prove it at my expense." Augusta remembered the experience and couldn't help but giggle in spite of herself. "I wish I'd seen my face when he came into the hotel lounge and you introduced us."

Mal's eyes twinkled as he pulled her close. "The best man won. You left France and Jean-Luc behind…and eventually walked into my life. For which I am eternally grateful."

"You know you're the love of my life, and you've given me this lovely family to top it off. Max is the icing on the cake."

Malcolm grinned broadly. "He's special, isn't he? I doubt you have any idea how happy it makes me that we have all this together."

Augusta kissed him. "Actually, I believe I do."

***

The next morning, Mal and Augusta shared a breakfast tray he had prepared and brought up to their bedroom, and he again mentioned the Geller case.

"This morning Danny and Jim will plan their reinvestigation of Leon Booth's trip to Vegas. It's a slim lead, but it may take us closer to solving the case."

A sudden thought struck Augusta. "Mal, Titus asked about the case when Milly and I saw him yesterday. He remembers Gene Geller from Gene's college days. And there were times Titus substituted for the organist at Rockdale Temple when Gene was singing. One thing he mentioned…and it might be nothing at all…he drew a parallel between Gene and Wesley Vandergriff."

"In what way?"

"Another love triangle. Only in Gene's case, it was really more that another student at U.C. was trying to get Elena's attention. Titus mentioned Gene had an altercation with that young man." She took a bite of omelet. "Gene minored in music and was on the Conservatory campus a couple of days a week, I think. This other guy…Benjamin something…was pretty persistent until Gene shut him down one day at the Conservatory. Then Titus said he heard the guy left before finishing his degree."

"So that would have been over twenty years ago."

"Yes, and Titus also said he never saw the man again once he'd left. He thought he went back to his home somewhere in the south. He also couldn't recall the last name…started with an 'R,' though. Roberts, Richards…something like that."

140

"You know, that's an angle that hadn't occurred to me—it appears that lover boy Geller left behind a trail of brokenhearted women and angry men, but this was an instance of a jealous would-be rival. I wonder if there have been other men interested in Elena more recently. And if she possibly responded to anyone."

"I seriously doubt that." Augusta finished her coffee. "She was crazy about Gene. You know, I have a friend in U.C. administration who could probably check the records to find Benjamin's last name if you think it's worth looking into."

"Well, if he were still in the area, it might be. But since he's long gone, I doubt it would lead us anywhere."

"Yes, that's true." *Still…it wouldn't hurt to find the name*, she thought. *You never know where you might find a puzzle piece.*

Mal left for City Hall to meet with Jim and Danny. "I should be home for dinner, but you know the drill…I can't make any promises. We never know what might happen in our 'city with eight thousand stories'."

"Eight thousand? The announcer on 'Naked City' said eight million."

"Yeah, but that was New York," Mal laughed.

Augusta took advantage of an especially beautiful fall morning. She took Fritz for a long walk before leaving early for the Conservatory in order to phone the friend at U.C. she had mentioned to Mal.

"Lucy, when you have a chance, could you check your records for a Benjamin, last name begins with R, something like Roberts or Richards, during the years

141

1941-44? He left before finishing his degree, after the first semester of his junior year, I believe."

A tap on her door, and Milly stuck her head in. Augusta waved to her to enter. "Great! Thanks so much."

Augusta hung up the phone and smiled at Milly. "That was Lucy Gravetz at U.C. I'm curious about Elena's unwanted suitor from her college days and asked Lucy if she can track his records down. She says she has some free time and she'll get back to me as soon as she finds something about Benjamin Roberts, or whatever his last name was."

"Well, that was propitious," Milly said. "I'll hang around for a bit to see where this goes." She plopped down in a chair and relaxed. "You'd have been teaching here when Gene was in school. You don't remember him back then?"

"I do, of course. Gene was certainly someone people were aware of. But he didn't study with me, and I don't recall that he was involved in any Conservatory performing organizations. I remember seeing him a few times, and hearing him once or twice on a class recital."

"Did you know Elena?"

"Not really. I may have seen her at those recitals when he performed. Wonder what Benjamin Last-Name-Beginning-With-R studied at U.C.?"

In a surprisingly brief time the phone rang, and Augusta answered, taking copious notes on a pad as she spoke with Lucy. "Thanks so much, Lucy. I owe you one."

"It looks like she found him. Benjamin Rodgers. He was in school at U.C. for two years and one semester."

Milly studied the pad Augusta handed her. "Political science major. Since he was eighteen in 1941 when he enrolled, he'd be forty-four now. I see he came from Montgomery, Alabama. Wonder if he went back there after he left Cincinnati?"

"He would have lost his student deferment when he left school, so he might well have been drafted to serve in World War II."

"Well, that's all very interesting, but I can't see that it's one bit of help in solving Gene's murder," Milly commented.

"Probably not." Augusta thought for a minute. "But I wonder if Titus really had the whole story? Maybe there was more to the Elena-Benjamin romance that he didn't know about."

Milly folded her arms across her chest. "Hmm, I wonder if Elena would like to have lunch one day soon?"

Chapter 13
The First Test

October 31

While there had been no more anonymous mail since Friday, twice over the weekend and again on Monday Augusta received phone calls possibly from the same person. Breathing at the other end of the line and then an abrupt *click* as the receiver was hung up on the other end. *How childish,* was her reaction. *This feels more and more like some unhappy student trying to get a rise out of me. Well, I refuse to be intimidated any longer.* She decided not to mention the calls to Malcolm.

Augusta enjoyed a leisurely drive from Cliffside to the Conservatory late Tuesday afternoon, winding through some side roads. She parked on Highland Avenue, about a block from the main entrance to the Conservatory, and walked up to the side door. She planned to stop by her studio before meeting her opera cast in Recital Hall for a read-through of the first act of the Mozart opera.

She gathered up the cast list, her score, and a pad for making notes, and was about to leave the studio when the phone rang.

"Augusta McKee."

A pause, and then the phone went dead. "Well, happy Halloween to you, too," she snapped into the dead phone.

This is ridiculous. She phoned the switchboard. "Was the call I just received cut off for some reason?"

"The caller ended it, Professor McKee," the student operator told her.

"I see. Was it an outside call or from inside the building?"

"Outside call."

Augusta shook off her annoyance and headed for Recital Hall. Stacy caught up with her.

"This is exciting for me, Augusta. But I guess it's different after you've done it a few times."

"Not really," Augusta smiled at her choreographer. "I'm excited about this project, too. Something a bit different. And always, a new cast, and the opportunity to help performers grow and hone their craft. Honestly, I live for this."

Re-acquainting herself with the text of the opera, Augusta had spotted a number of items she changed or cut. *There's far too much dialogue, and some is from another culture and a long-ago time.* Monostatos had "slaves" who were now "servants." *Maybe I'm being overly sensitive, but it's a fairy tale*, Augusta thought. *We don't need slaves.*

She also removed the element of misogyny by changing the lines in which Tamino and Papageno are instructed not to talk to women, they were instead to take a vow of silence. Augusta was aware this was a common change made in contemporary productions. *A lesson in self-discipline.* It was especially difficult for Tamino because Pamina was heartbroken when the man of her dreams whom she had finally met greeted her with silence.

She laughed aloud when considering the directive to Papageno. *Papageno is such a goofball he'll talk too much to anybody, so he won't be able to follow any kind of instructions where talking is concerned.*

The cast and directors were called for this rehearsal at six in the evening which meant the students had time for dinner before reporting. As the scores to the opera were passed out, Augusta explained they would see some changes in the text. "I want this to be an uplifting, positive experience for all of us, performers and audience alike. And always keep in mind, since *The Magic Flute* is an allegory, the places, events, and even characters can represent an abstract idea."

Angelica lifted a hand and Augusta recognized her. "Like my character, 'The Queen of the Night.' She's the epitome of a 'bad guy' type who confuses people because she pretends to be virtuous."

"Exactly," Augusta nodded approvingly. "So when she is vanquished at the end of the opera, it's not really the character being removed from the world, but what she represents."

Leroy waved a hand in the air. "Yeah, but what about my character, Papageno? He's a 'bird-man,' which I guess means I get to wear a cool costume." Laughter from all.

"Oh, undoubtedly," Augusta chuckled. "Think about it, Leroy. He's humorous, impulsive, loyal, kind-hearted, a little goofy, and brave even when he's scared. Don't we all know people who fill that description?"

"He's also looking for love in all the wrong places," Denise observed. "And the first thing he does when he comes onstage is brag to Tamino that he killed the serpent when we just saw the Three Ladies do away with it."

"So, I guess he's kind of an 'Everyman,' in a way," Leroy said. He rubbed his hands together. "I can do brave when I'm scared. This is gonna be fun." More laughter.

Augusta glanced at the piano, where Byron Matthias was turning pages for their pianist, Miriam Levengood. "Maestro Matthias won't be formally conducting today, but if there's a lengthy interlude, he may throw you a cue. There really aren't many, since much of the action takes place during dialogue scenes."

She glanced around at her cast, who seemed excited and eager to begin this journey. "We won't listen to the entire overture, which is about eight or nine minutes long, but let's do listen to the opening chords and the final section, please."

For the next two hours, the performers and their directors immersed themselves in Mozart's opera. Without being directed to, each stood whenever their role called for them to sing or deliver spoken lines, the others listening attentively and reacting to their fellow cast members. *Already thinking about their characters,* Augusta thought.

Augusta made notes about a few musical cuts, and also about dialogue that still seemed somewhat awkward. The set began to grow in her mind from the few initial thoughts she'd had. Stacy Mathis, their choreographer, busily made notes as well, glancing at Augusta occasionally with a big smile as she heard performers read with animation and expression.

At the end of the rehearsal, Augusta's colleagues expressed their appreciation for the enthusiastic young cast. "So sorry John Edmanston couldn't make it tonight," Byron added.

"He was as well," Augusta replied. "I hope he recovers from his bronchitis quickly. That's such a nasty illness."

"We have another meeting Thursday night for Act Two, correct?" Stacy asked. "Then one final session next Tuesday before taking a break until January."

"Yes, correct," Augusta answered. "The cast is expected to memorize their roles during that down time so that when we get back together in January, they're ready for the staging rehearsals." Glancing around, she saw all of the cast had exited Recital Hall. She collected her materials and placed them in her briefcase, closing and locking it.

"Byron…would you mind walking me to my car? I'm just about a block down Highland Avenue."

Augusta was reluctant to ask, but she had promised Malcolm she wouldn't walk to her car by herself after dark. It made sense, but it also made her feel a little helpless. *After all, I do have my gun in my briefcase. Still, I promised.*

"Yes, I know. I parked about two cars behind yours, so I'm headed that way anyhow."

They chatted as they strolled down to their cars. "You have a good cast for this opera, Augusta," Byron commented. "We should have an unusually fine production, because I know we'll see some fascinating stuff on stage."

"I still have to sit down with Larry Rogers and discuss the set. I have some new ideas after tonight. I think a unit set may work, with a few items to be moved on and off for certain scenes."

They arrived at her car and Augusta fished her keys from her bag. "I know we only see it briefly, but I want a fantastic serpent in the beginning. Something to really grab the audience's attention."

"Larry may have something in his bag of tricks. I know he builds items for a good many theaters all over the tri-state area."

"He may indeed, or something that can be rebuilt into my dream serpent."

Byron held the door as Augusta settled herself, then closed it firmly after wishing her goodnight. She took a few minutes to relax and reflect before turning the key to the ignition, waving to Byron as he drove past her on his way home.

She turned on the lights and pulled forward, heading for the traffic light at Highland and East

McMillan as it changed from red to green. As she turned right, she tapped on the brakes to slow slightly.

They didn't respond. She pressed her foot down more firmly. And then again. And again. Still nothing.

"Why won't...my brakes aren't working," she said aloud. Her eyes darted around the street at the moving cars on this busy road, aware of them as never before. Her back and shoulders clenched as she felt a wave of cold flow through her and she gasped for air. Augusta clutched the steering wheel and instinctively used the horn to warn other drivers.

What do I do? Her foot was carefully away from the accelerator. The road was level, and there wasn't a huge amount of traffic. *Lights.* Teeth chattering, she flipped on the hazard lights. She swallowed, feeling her throat begin to close up. *Emergency brake.* She reached for it and jerked it up, causing the car to swerve and nearly hit another automobile, its horn blaring as it sped away.

A patrol car headed in the opposite direction passed. With considerable effort, Augusta pressed the horn repeatedly as she straightened the car, praying they would hear and turn around.

One final thing...downshift. Get the car into first gear. She spotted an open stretch of parking spaces to her right and headed for it, getting close enough to scrape the tires and fender on the passenger side of the car as it continued to slow. She moved even closer to the curb and finally felt the car shudder to a stop. Shaking, she turned off the ignition and leaned her arms and head against the steering wheel.

Relief flooded through her as she fought back tears. A tap at the window showed the anxious face of a young patrolman. Augusta wiped her eyes and opened the door.

"Ma'am, are you okay? We saw you had lost control of your car." He looked again. "Mrs. Mitchell?"

"Yes, Officer. I'm grateful you stopped." Augusta took a shaky breath. "That was terrifying, my brakes weren't working at all."

"Mrs. Mitchell, I think I should get in touch with Lieutenant Mitchell and ask him what he wants us to do. We'll stay here with you."

"Yes, I'd appreciate that." The patrolman rushed to his car and spoke with his partner, quickly returning to Augusta.

"It's chilly, Mrs. Mitchell. Why don't you come and wait in our car?"

"I think I will," Augusta replied. "I can't understand why that would happen. I had the car inspected and serviced only a couple of weeks ago." She pulled the briefcase from the car and the keys from the ignition. "I know it's four years old, but I've taken the best possible care of it. Thank you, Officer…?"

"Jack Reynolds, ma'am."

He gently took her elbow and escorted her to the patrol car, opening the door as she slid in and tried to relax. "This is my partner, Dave Baldwin."

"Lieutenant Mitchell is on his way, ma'am," Officer Baldwin told her. "Are you sure you're not hurt?"

"No, thankfully, I was driving fairly slowly."

"We clocked you at about 25mph, but that's fast when you don't have brakes. When did you realize they weren't responding?"

"I just turned off Highland Avenue a few blocks back, and realized after I turned right that my brakes were...weren't working. It was the first time I'd applied—or tried to apply—the brakes since I got in the car."

"Mrs. Mitchell tells me she just had the car inspected and serviced," Jack Reynolds told his partner. "Only a few weeks ago."

Augusta noticed a glance pass between them. "May I see your keys, Mrs. Mitchell?" She passed them to Reynolds. "Be right back."

This could have had a very bad ending, Augusta thought, hugging herself, unable to stop shaking. She saw the flashing light on Mal's car approaching. *That was fast, thank goodness.* He wasn't driving a patrol car but had a light in his car that could quickly be affixed to the roof and used when necessary. Obviously he had thought it necessary.

Before joining her, Malcolm strode to her car to speak with Officer Reynolds. The two of them knelt beside the car for a few minutes.

Mal jerked open the car door and slid in beside her, gently taking her hands. "Scary thing to have happened, Augusta," he said, fighting to control his voice. "You seem to be fine."

"Shaky, but in one piece."

"Good job of stopping the car. You did good. And it was lucky these two patrolmen saw you and came back to check on you."

"Yes, I certainly appreciated that. But…what about my car, Mal? I'm sure I did some damage the way I slid along the curb."

"I need to get you home. Don't worry about your car right now. I'm going to ask Officers Reynolds and Baldwin to wait here while we have it picked up and towed to be examined."

"Why on earth would you do that?" Augusta stared at him, again feeling the cold begin to creep through her.

Mal's grip on her hands tightened. "The brake cable was cut, Gus. This is way beyond anonymous notes."

Chapter 14
A Vengeance Aria

Once in Mal's car, wrapped in his strong, warm arms, Augusta gave in to the emotions she'd been keeping under tight control.

"I was so…so, *so scared*," she choked out. "I'm sorry, I don't mean to be such a baby."

"Let it out, Gus. I'm sure it was terrifying," he soothed.

A few more tears, then a hiccupy sigh. "It was awful."

"You could have been killed."

She pulled back and gazed at him. "I could have killed someone else. That's one thing that I kept thinking."

"But you didn't," he said firmly. "You managed to keep the car under control and bring it to a stop."

He turned on the ignition. "Let's get you home. You should take a warm bath and relax."

He drove slowly, Augusta's head on his shoulder. *I'm exhausted*, she thought. Neither of them spoke again until they were in the house. Fritz greeted them at the door but seemed subdued as if suspecting something was not right. Augusta bent down and petted him, and he whined softly.

"I'll take him out for a few minutes. Go upstairs and undress, and I'll draw your bath."

Augusta nodded and slowly climbed the stairs. Everything in her house seemed especially wonderful to her. *I might never have seen any of this again*, she thought with a shudder. She undressed, pulled a dressing gown across her shoulders, and turned on the water in the tub.

Malcolm joined her, helping her step into the tub. He took a bath sponge and soap in hand, sat on the edge of the tub, and bathed her as if she were a child.

He wrapped a towel around Augusta as she stepped out of the tub. "I put on coffee when I came in. Why don't I bring us each a mug? Or would you rather have wine?"

"No, coffee sounds wonderful. Thank you."

She slipped into the gown and climbed into bed, piling pillows behind her, determined to relax and put what she had just experienced out of her mind.

Mal returned with a tray holding their coffee and a plate of biscotti.

"Oh, good, you found them. I was just thinking I could do with some sugar, along with the caffeine. I'll be myself in no time."

Mal removed his shoes and joined her on the bed. "There's my fiery gypsy. But we have to talk."

Augusta bit into a cookie. "I know I'm not going to like this."

"No, you aren't." A gentle hand on her chin, tipping her face toward his. "Augusta, someone just tried to kill you."

"Yes, I'm very much aware of that, Lieutenant Mitchell…believe me. Does this mean you're going to assign a detail to me, which I really do not want you to do? You're all so busy with the Gene Geller case."

"I wish it were that simple." A swallow of coffee. "If you had witnessed a crime and the criminal were still on the loose, that would justify me assigning two detectives out of our department total of ten to guard you. At this point, we suspect someone could be targeting you. The forensic examination of your car may give us more evidence. It seems highly unlikely, but it's possible it could have been a senseless, random act."

"So we just wait to see if something else happens?"

"Hardly. I need for you to stay put until we find who did this. In other words, I need to know where you are at all times. Don't go anywhere without contacting me first."

"Stay put? You mean stay at home? You know I can't do that. I have a full schedule. I have people I need to see and who need to see me."

"That's how it has to be, Gus."

"You're asking me to stay home and wonder if the lowlife who cut my brake cable is going to show up in broad daylight and attack me right here in my own home? Even though he snuck around after dark to do what he did tonight?"

Augusta firmly placed her coffee mug on the tray and sat up straight. "I honestly think I'm safer at the school, where there are a lot of people around."

He gazed at her, his jaw set, worry in his eyes. *Oh, those eyes. I don't like seeing them so troubled, though.*

"I told you before, I can take care of myself," she said.

Mal continued to gaze at her, but his expression changed. "I'll drive you to the Conservatory before I go to City Hall. And either pick you up myself or arrange for Dan or Jim to do that. I'll agree to try that for the present."

"I hope we find the person quickly who did this." Augusta nibbled on a second biscotti. "I'm sure you're right, it was *not* a disgruntled student. But who could it have been?"

"Your car will be thoroughly examined at the lab. We may find fingerprints. A handprint. Maybe another clue. We'll find the scumbag."

Malcolm removed the tray and again took Augusta in his arms, holding her close.

"I'm okay, Mal. Truly." She pulled back. "And tonight, I'm perfectly content to 'stay put.' I like it here…in your arms."

She snuggled closer to him. "Come to bed," she murmured.

***

"I understand this is necessary, but it feels strange. You seem to think I need a bodyguard." They were approaching the Conservatory.

"My dear, you live with a bodyguard." Mal gave her a crooked grin.

"Well, now that you put it that way, I guess I do. And I've put him to the test more than once. I'll try to avoid doing that again."

"It wouldn't surprise me to learn that word has spread through this community that an attempt was made on Professor McKee's life last night."

"That's entirely possible. It's also possible a student who lives in the area may have even seen my car parked oddly and a patrol car nearby, and there could already be a lot of speculation. How do you suggest I handle that?"

"Don't mention it…after you talk to Milly, which I know will be the first thing you do. And Garrett may well have already told her."

"Garrett. Knows all, sees all, tells Milly all." She thought for a moment. "Well, if anyone mentions it, how about this: I tell them I had a problem with my car and it had to be towed, but luckily, I wasn't hurt."

"Perfect. Hopefully, it will only be for a few days, Augusta," Mal said as she opened the car door.

Some of her students entered the studio tentatively. Augusta spoke to each of them cheerfully as if it were a perfectly normal day. The only one who addressed the situation was, not surprisingly, George Van Dorn.

"Professor McKee, there's a lot of talk this morning about a couple of people seeing you sitting in a police car last night and your car was parked at a funny angle across the street. As if there had been an accident."

"Well, there almost was, George. I had a mechanical problem but was able to stop the car. It was towed and Lieutenant Mitchell came and picked me up. Luckily, I was not hurt, but I'm without a car for the present."

George gazed at her skeptically. "Well…if that's all it was.…"

"I'm fine, George. Don't give it a second thought. My husband will probably be bringing me to school for another day or two until the car is repaired or I get a rental."

The morning passed quickly. Augusta had not had time to speak with Milly before her lessons started, but climbed the steps to Milly's studio before lunch.

"I heard," Milly said, hugging her. "You look okay."

"I'm fine…I think. I hope I never have that happen to me again. Very, very frightening."

"I wondered if I'd see you today. Garrett was sure Mal would have wanted you to stay home."

"We had a discussion," Augusta smirked. "Guess what. I won. At least for today."

"Do you think this could be the same person who's been sending anonymous notes?"

"Oh, I do. And the hang-up calls."

"You didn't tell me about those."

"I mainly ignored them. I was convinced it was…how did you put it? Some snarky soprano who was passed over for a big role in *The Magic Flute*. Now, I don't know what to think. Milly, it was so frightening."

More lessons after lunch, the last one with Denise James. Denise, a usually ebullient young woman, seemed subdued and Augusta thought she knew why.

"Denise, congratulations on being cast as Pamina. You're going to be exceptional in the role."

Denise stared at the floor, pressing her lips together. "I...I felt honored to have been cast. There were so many fine sopranos who auditioned."

"Look at me, Denise. You won that role. It was a unanimous decision by the audition board. Don't think for one second you didn't deserve the role."

Augusta saw tears in her student's eyes. "Professor McKee...there's been some talk...."

"Denise, listen to me. Pay no attention to any gossipy nonsense you hear. Every role in this production was filled solely based on artistic and vocal merit."

A slight smile. "Thank you, Professor McKee. I really appreciate hearing that. And most people have been very supportive."

Augusta handed her a tissue and smiled. "Take a deep breath and relax, Denise. Let's get started."

After Denise's lesson ended at three-thirty, Augusta put the music away, wiped the piano with a soft cloth, and covered the keyboard, preparing to leave. She assumed the tap on her door was Danny or Jim, arriving to take her home. Instead, she saw a flustered Eloise Heinlein, the somewhat obnoxious member of the Conservatory's Board of Directors.

"Eloise? Can I help you with something?"

"May I come in? I need to talk with you."

"Certainly."

Once seated, Eloise seemed distraught, twisting a hankie she pulled from her bag.

"I heard about what happened last night. I hope you're all right. I thought I might see a detective nearby."

"I'm fine, really. There's no need for that. It was just a near-accident when my brakes failed. Fortunately, I managed to keep the car under control, but I sure hope it never happens to me again."

"That must have been frightening, and here's why I'm concerned about what happened to you." Eloise blotted her face. "I went to see Barry Whittier in prison this morning. I think I told you I visit him from time to time."

"Yes, you did." Augusta paused. "How is he?"

"He was…strange." She paused, fishing for words. "I've never seen him quite the way he was this morning. He wanted to talk about you, Augusta."

Augusta stared at her. "In what way?"

"At first he was sad, talking about Anton Portnov…you remember him, the cellist Barry was in love with who died in an automobile accident a couple of years ago."

"Yes, I do remember." *Where is this going?*

"Then he got very worked up. He talked about how he ended up in prison, but a lot of it made no sense at all." She touched the hankie to her upper lip and cheeks. "The thing is…he blames you for him being there. He said more than once 'it's all Augusta McKee's fault. If she had minded her own business, I wouldn't be here.'"

"Barry Whittier is in prison because he killed two people, Eloise. That was a choice he made. A terrible choice."

"I realize that. There was a guard with us who finally brought an end to the…conversation, if you can call it that…and escorted me out." Another dab of her face with the handkerchief.

"It was frightening to hear him talk that way. I've never seen him like that. I'm not sure I'll go back. The man is mentally unbalanced."

"I would agree with you there. I believe you said he's receiving treatment, though."

"Yes, he's receiving treatment, but what happened today makes me wonder if he's just going through the motions and pretending he wants help."

She paused, staring at the window. "One thing he said I thought I should tell you, and you may want to pass it on to Lieutenant Mitchell."

Augusta listened attentively.

"He said, 'Augusta McKee thinks she's safe because I'm in prison. She should remember I have powerful friends on the outside.' That was frightening."

"Yes, it was." Augusta felt a chill. *Is it possible Barry Whittier could have had something to do with what happened to me last night?*

Eloise replaced her handkerchief and snapped her bag shut. "I thought I should come over and tell you this in person. And I waited until I knew you didn't have any more students for the day." She stood, preparing to leave.

Augusta walked her to the door. "I appreciate this, Eloise. And I'll definitely let the police know about Barry's threat."

"Of course, he could have just been blowing off steam. He *is* a writer, you know, and no doubt has a vivid imagination. He could be delusional, too."

Or there could be some truth in what he said. I know some criminals have a network beyond prison walls, Augusta thought.

"Thank you again, Eloise. This couldn't have been easy."

"Yes. Well, I hope to see you under better circumstances soon."

Another tap at her door, and it was Danny, who nodded to Eloise as she breezed past him. He lifted a quizzical eyebrow at Augusta. "Any more students, meetings, or anything else, or are you ready to go? Jim's waiting out front."

"Just let me grab my coat and purse, and we can leave."

Once in the car, Augusta told them both about Eloise's visit to Barry Whittier. "Should we go to headquarters and give this information to Mal? I know it may just be Whittier being grandiose, but on the other hand...."

Jim headed for downtown Cincinnati. "On the other hand, the man has money. We can't ignore this, Augusta. We also know Whittier had criminal contacts in Europe when the murders were committed of the two members of the Chrysanthemum Quartet. Who can say what kind of contacts he might have here?"

Malcolm seemed surprised when the three of them walked into his office in City Hall.

"An unexpected pleasure. Or is it?" He hung Augusta's coat on a rack and they all sat down.

Augusta explained what Eloise Heinlein had told her. "You know what you said last night, about my brakes being tampered with going far beyond a disgruntled student? I don't think I understood how much Barry Whittier hates me. I had no idea he's dreamed up this idea that his imprisonment is my doing."

Augusta studied Mal's face. *Set jaw, eyes narrowed.* She thought of it as full detective mode; she could almost see the wheels turning.

He glanced around at each of them. "You were right to come and give me this information immediately. Obviously, Whittier couldn't have cut Augusta's brake cable himself, but it's true cons sometimes have strong contacts with criminals on the outside."

Augusta leaned forward. "So, it's possible what happened to me...even the notes and the phone calls...may have nothing at all to do with *The Magic Flute.*"

"Phone calls?" Mal's head jerked up.

"Hang-up calls. Several of them. I thought...I just ignored them. Maybe I shouldn't have."

Mal nodded. "Whittier's threat needs to be investigated thoroughly."

Chapter 15
The Guardians at the Gate?

It was late, but traffic on Interstate 75 was unusually heavy. Rain and wind only made driving more difficult, and Augusta slowed slightly and carefully stayed in the right lane. The car behind her was following too closely, and she signaled to pull into the left lane and eased into the flow of traffic. A sudden maneuver from the car ahead in the left lane caused her to step on the brakes.

The brakes didn't respond. And suddenly everything changed: she was on a four-lane highway with no median, and traffic moved toward her more and more quickly. The rain changed to heavy snow and she could barely see. Fear raced through her as she stepped repeatedly on the brakes, but they weren't responding. Suddenly headlights flooded her front windshield and....

Heart pounding, Augusta awoke, taking deep breaths. Warm, strong arms pulled her close and she clung to Mal.

"I've got you, Gus." He held her even more closely, stroking her back and shoulders. "That must have been one hell of a nightmare."

A deep sigh, pulled up from the depth of her being. "The worst I can ever remember."

He rocked her gently. "It may happen again, Gus. You went through an unimaginable ordeal Tuesday night."

Augusta leaned up on one elbow. "I thought I was okay. I've been trying to shake it off. And I've been through stuff before that didn't...didn't get to me as this has."

She lay down again and snuggled close to Mal. "The thing that's the worst...I could have killed somebody. If I hadn't been able to keep my car under control...and I was using everything I had to do that...someone else could have been killed. I can't get that out of my head."

Mal stroked her hair back from her face and gazed into her eyes. "I could have lost you. I'm having some trouble keeping that out of my head. I don't know what I'd do if that happened." He kissed her softly.

"I can't dwell on might have been." She shuddered. "A multiple-car accident. A fatal accident." She laughed shakily. "See what I mean? My mind just keeps going back to that. I think this is why it's important for me to keep to my usual schedule."

"It's going to take a while. And yes, I do understand. Keeping your life as 'normal' as possible does help."

Augusta grew quiet. "But you know...I think I will cancel my lessons at Cliffside tomorrow. Or is it today?"

Mal glanced at the clock. "It's two in the morning. So it's Thursday. How many students do you have there on Thursdays?"

"Only three. And Sister Mary Norbert can work with them on music, so they won't miss their lessons. But I do need to be at the Conservatory for lessons this morning, and then go back for the rehearsal tonight." Another sigh and she managed to relax against Mal's warmth and strength.

Once again, he gently stroked her shoulders and back. "Danny and Jim are all set to be on hand for that. It makes sense, and they're willing to do it."

"I don't like asking them to do this on their own time."

"They care about you, Gus. They'd be willing to do much more to keep you safe. I'd do it myself, except that I have to speak at that City Council meeting tonight."

Mal sat up. "Can I get you something to drink? Water? Maybe hot tea?"

Augusta realized she was parched. "Water sounds wonderful. Why am I so thirsty?"

"Stress. Want something else to help you relax? Maybe a couple of aspirin?"

"Not a bad idea. How do you know all this stuff? Wait, don't answer that. I know how. All those many years of dealing with similar experiences. First in the Marines, and for many years now as a law enforcement officer."

Augusta lay back and stared at the ceiling, trying to shake the effects of the nightmare and of what had caused it. *What would I do without my magnificent detective?* she thought. *How on earth did I manage to survive all those years without this man who has become my life?*

She smiled and sat up when Mal returned, Fritz at his heels. "Fritzy's worried about his mommy," Mal explained. "I think we could let him sleep by the bed, don't you?"

Augusta patted her dog's head and he curled up beside the bed, chin on paws as he stared fixedly at his mistress. "There's something I need to do on Friday, and I hope you can help me find a way to make it happen." She took the glass from Malcolm and sipped the water.

"I'm listening."

"Milly and I invited Elena Geller to lunch at the Vernon Manor." She held up a hand. "I know you won't want me to go into a public place where anyone could come and go. I'll talk to Milly tomorrow...well, later this morning...to see if she has any ideas. It's in the middle of a busy day for both of us, but there must be some option."

"Can't you just postpone your lunch date?"

"We could. But the main purpose of this is to find out more about Elena's old beau. We learned his name...Benjamin Rodgers...and that he left Cincinnati after he dropped out of U.C. midway through his junior year. We wondered if there might be more to that situation than Titus was aware of."

"Benjamin Rodgers. Any relation to Larry Rogers, your set designer?"

"Highly doubtful. Different spelling. And it is a fairly common surname. Milly and I speculated that

Benjamin Rodgers might have been drafted since the war wasn't over yet. Or he may have returned to Alabama, which is where he was from."

Mal thought for a moment. "Can you invite Elena to your studio and have food delivered? One of us could be on hand when the delivery is made."

"That sounds like an option. Milly's studio would be more comfortable. It's quite a bit larger than mine, and she even keeps a folding table in the room for meetings.

"And you know," Augusta added, "That might be even better. In a private space with just the three of us there, Elena may very well open up more."

Mal took the glass and eased Augusta onto her back. "Well, now that we've solved your immediate problems, try to get some sleep, bride. Six-thirty isn't far off."

***

Augusta slept surprisingly well for the next few hours and woke just before six-thirty. She reached for the alarm and silenced it, turning back to see Mal just opening his eyes.

Oh, those eyes. Even at the beginning, when he was annoying me thoroughly by keeping me off the Cliffside campus, those intense dark blue eyes had me. She leaned over and kissed each one softly.

"Gus…I have to get up and go to work." His voice sounded husky.

"I know. And first, you have to drop me off at the Conservatory." She caressed his face. "Mal…let's go

171

away after all this is over. Just the two of us. For at least two weeks. We haven't really had that kind of trip since our honeymoon, and that was two and a half years ago."

He grinned and leaned up on an elbow. "Any idea where you want to take this second honeymoon, Mrs. Mitchell?"

"Canada. Montreal and points north first. Then take the train across the continent through the Rockies and visit Vancouver, where I've never been. Maybe travel to Seattle…I haven't been there either…and fly home from there." Augusta sat up and hugged her knees. "You can practice your French in Quebec. We can discover Vancouver together."

"Something to think about. We'll talk more when things settle down."

Mal gave her a quick kiss when he drove her to the Conservatory entrance. "What time are you finished? If I can't pick you up I'll ask Jim or Dan to be here."

"Let's say twelve-thirty. My last lesson is over at noon."

Milly had picked up her mail and was heading for her studio when Augusta breezed into Main Hall. "Oh, good. Can you come to my studio for a few minutes? There's something I need to discuss with you."

"I can." Milly accompanied her down the hall. Augusta's studio was on the first floor of the addition to Main Hall, built to accommodate mostly private studios but also containing three small classrooms. In the basement below were numerous practice rooms, a laundry room for residents, and the school library which was quickly outgrowing the space. Two studios contained small pipe organs where lessons were conducted. One had been named the "Titus Powlett Organ Studio" in honor of that esteemed instructor and organist.

"What's up?" Milly asked. She examined Augusta critically. "I think what happened the other night is wearing on you. You look as if you didn't get much sleep last night."

"Is it that bad?" Augusta removed a compact from her bag and opened it, peering into the small mirror and pressing make-up under her eyes. "Well, there's not much I can do about it. Hopefully, my students aren't as observant as you are. I'm sure they won't care."

"You're fine. And it's only because I've known you for most of your life that I notice this stuff. Anyway, what did you need to talk to me about?"

Augusta explained the idea she had for their planned luncheon with Elena.

"I have an even better idea," Milly said. "I'll ask the cafeteria staff to prepare something nice for us and bring it up to my studio. I just need to think what I can bribe them with."

"That's perfect. That way the CPD won't need to have a detective on hand to oversee the delivery. Well, maybe not oversee it...but be on hand when it happens. You're a genius."

"Let's just hope Elena tells us something that will help the CPD find her husband's killer. That doesn't seem very likely, though."

"It's a long shot...but sometimes a puzzle piece shows up totally unexpectedly. Remember Linnea's case? I looked at a photo of Linnea that reminded me of a student I had years ago who had died young. There was an almost eerie resemblance. And that eventually led Mal to Linnea's murderer."

Augusta's first lesson that morning was Denise James. Vocal performance majors received two half-hour lessons a week, which were included in their program and covered by their tuition. In contrast to her previous lesson, Denise was in high spirits and eager for the rehearsal that night.

Taking Denise through her vocal warmups, Augusta thought for a moment about what precisely she did to help a young singer to become a skilled singer. *Most people have no idea how much work this is*, she thought. *The vocal mechanism is made up of many muscles, and a singer needs to be as disciplined and aware of their body as an athlete is. And then make it all look and sound easy. It's a lifetime of care for their instrument. And then add the passion and beauty of the music they love and are privileged to perform. There's nothing like it.*

Denise, flushed with the particularly successful lesson she'd just experienced, gazed at her teacher. "I learned some new things today. That was so much fun. I can't wait to practice. Thank you, Professor McKee."

"Excellent lesson, Denise. I'm looking forward to tonight."

And that's what it's all about. What happens to her in the future depends on so much, but I'm giving her many of the tools she'll need. She recalled the words of a former student, a young baritone now enjoying success throughout Europe: "It's too bad singers…well, all musicians, really…can't minor in Luck." *The one thing I can't give Denise. I can teach her how to use her voice correctly so that it will last her entire life, and encourage the passion she already has. But Luck is always the unknown element in a career.*

She finished a little early and went to the entrance to await her bodyguard, whoever it might be, and was pleased to see it was Mal.

"Oh, good. I'd hoped it might be you." The aroma of food immediately hit her when she sat down next to him. "Oh, and you stopped at Skyline. You are the best."

"I can't stay after we eat. But I'll be your bodyguard whenever I'm able."

Fritz greeted them effusively when they entered the house, and the chili was quickly placed on plates and Lieutenant and Mrs. Mitchell sat down in the alcove for lunch.

"Do you remember the first time we ever enjoyed Skyline Chili together?" Augusta asked between bites.

"I do. It was when we were working on the Linnea Murphy case. You had a scare and I took you to Skyline because you hadn't had anything to eat that evening."

"And you told me why you became a homicide detective. Because you thought it was one of the most cognitively satisfying things on earth to find the person who had done harm to another person. No, to more than one person…potentially to many people, unless you could stop them."

Mal grinned as he dumped the rest of his chili onto his plate. "You remember all that?"

"Of course, I do." Augusta took a swallow of iced tea. "And you brought me home and kissed me. Our first kiss."

Mal took a final bite of his Skyline Chili. "And luckily for me…we haven't stopped since."

Augusta chuckled as he wiped his mouth and hands, stood, and pushed his chair in. "Don't worry about the dishes. I know you have to get back to your office."

"Yes, I do. Danny and Jim are all set to be your bodyguards at tonight's rehearsal. What time do you want them to pick you up?"

"Six-fifteen would be great. Oh, is it okay if I take Fritz for a walk?"

"Sorry, Gus. I need you to stay in the house, and I walked him before I picked you up. Get a nap. Listen to music. I understand Mozart wrote this pretty nifty opera called…give me a minute. Oh, yes. *Die Zauberflöte*."

"Show-off."

"There may even be a recording stashed around here somewhere," Mal laughed as he headed for the door, Fritz at his heels.

Augusta caught up with him for a kiss and an embrace.

Please, keep him safe.

Chapter 16
The First Lady...Again

There were two entrances to Recital Hall at the Conservatory. An exterior entrance on Oak Street, across from the Vernon Manor Hotel, and a Conservatory interior entrance. When the extension to Main Hall was built, the architects connected it to Recital Hall as well. Stairs descending to the cafeteria were opposite the interior entrance. On bad weather days, students who lived in the women's dormitory could choose to take meals, classes, and lessons without ever needing to be outside.

Jim and Danny parked their car on the corner of Highland Avenue and Oak Street and walked with Augusta to the side entrance to Main Hall. That would be the only means of entry for anyone attending the rehearsal that night—entering through that door and going through the school to the interior entrance to the Recital Hall. The night watchman, an elderly gentleman known affectionately as "Pop," was on duty beginning at six p.m. The two detectives introduced themselves to him and then made themselves scarce. Augusta knew they would be close by, periodically glancing through the windowed double doors of the interior entryway.

The first order of business, once the cast had assembled, belonged to Stacy. She had invited six sopranos for a more intensive dance audition to select the actress for the role of Papagena.

"This wasn't easy. All of you are excellent dancers, and I want to thank you for such a great audition." She glanced around the cast. "But after a sleepless night and careful consideration, I'm happy to offer the role of Papagena to Hana Watanabe."

Applause and whistles from the cast for an obviously popular choice. Hana, flushed with excitement, stood and turned to her cast members, bowing gracefully, tears in her eyes. Augusta was delighted, knowing how well-liked the petite Japanese American junior had become during her time at the school. *Now we have a true multi-ethnic cast. I had hoped Hana would get the role.*

While the character Sarastro was introduced to the audience at the end of act one, Allan Meissner's first opportunity to sing one of his big arias was at the opening of act two. Many in the cast were not in school during the time Allan was there as an undergraduate student and had no idea of the power and beauty of this man's voice. They responded enthusiastically to hearing him, and Allan smiled and nodded briefly.

Vietnam has changed him, made him more reserved and thoughtful, Augusta thought, remembering the enthusiastic and delightful young man who had been an important part of the opera program before he enlisted in the Marines. *From what I hear, Vietnam changes every person who goes there.*

The rehearsal continued, with Tamino and Papageno tasked with observing a "trial of silence" and cautioned against speaking. Leroy had a great time totally ignoring all the admonitions, and Augusta realized she could incorporate his innate sense of comedy into the antics of their "Bird-man."

The cast paid close attention when Angelica sang through her big aria, the "Vengeance" aria which had won her the role of the Queen. More applause, this time with whistles and stomping. Augusta applauded with them, pleased at the show of enthusiasm for Angelica and for the opera they were tasked with bringing to the public. She had never directed this Mozart opera, or even been a cast member, and it surprised her to learn it was one of the three most performed operas worldwide. *I guess I'm about to find out why it's so popular,* she thought.

Denise was next, singing her beautiful, heart-wrenching aria, "Ach, ich fühl's." She performed it flawlessly and with considerable emotion. The cast paid close attention and to Augusta's delight they stood to applaud her. Denise had tears in her eyes as she acknowledged the support of her colleagues.

Denise is more than a soloist in this opera, Augusta thought. *I think the cast appreciates what she represents, a break with a bad tradition—a door opening and fresh air rushing in.*

She gave her cast a brief break, cautioning them not to venture beyond the side lobby. Allan sat quietly by himself, and Augusta joined him.

He smiled at her. "Denise James is exceptional. What a beautiful voice, and she sings that aria pretty much perfectly, don't you think?"

"Yes, she is something. And you—you're singing so well. What a treat to hear you again. It's good to be back, isn't it?"

He smiled gratefully. "More than I hope you'll ever understand."

"I've heard some reports about Vietnam that are disturbing in many different ways. I'm so happy you came back to us."

She saw his jaw work. "Not as glad as I am to be here. I just want to concentrate on singing and not think too much about that part of my life."

Yes, I've heard that before about Vietnam veterans. "Well…if you ever want to talk…I'm a good listener."

"Thank you, Professor."

The remainder of the rehearsal went smoothly. As the cast prepared to leave, Augusta noticed Denise James and George Van Horn engaged in an animated conversation. *There does seem to be some attraction there*, she thought. *I wonder how Denise's parents would feel about those two becoming involved. George's parents would probably welcome Denise, she's lovely.*

George excused himself and moved toward Augusta. "Professor McKee…you know I met some Cincinnati policemen in August when we were at Detective Headquarters," he said in a low voice. "I just want to say it's nice to feel protected. To know you're being protected."

"I'd appreciate your keeping that to yourself."

"Absolutely." He glanced at Denise. "Thanks for giving me this wonderful opportunity. I'm really looking forward to this show."

Augusta put a hand on his wrist. "George, would you do something for me? I know you've just met Allan Meissner, but he doesn't know many people in the cast. It would be great if you'd find a way to befriend him."

George grinned broadly. "He's so awesome he almost scares me. Are you sure he's not the real Sarastro?" They both chuckled. "But sure, I'll do that. I know he was in the military. My uncle is, too. In fact, he's been in Vietnam for nearly a year."

"Don't tell this to anybody, George, because you know I don't 'play favorites.'" Augusta returned the smile. "But you are just the best."

***

Milly's plan to have the cafeteria play caterer for their luncheon with Elena worked better than Augusta had anticipated. She gazed at the beautifully set table and the elegant food and stared at her friend. There was also a side table with dessert and coffee waiting.

"Okay, what was the bribe? I had no idea our cafeteria staff could put something like this together."

I got them tickets to *Mame* at the Schubert Theater next month." Milly chortled. "Garrett has connections."

"Of course, he does. Why don't you and I go? Maybe drag Garrett and Mal?"

"Mal would be shocked to know you want to see a Broadway musical." Milly moved around the table, straightening napkins and water glasses.

"I doubt that. Remember, I was directing *The Pirate of Penzance* when we met."

"That's not Broadway."

"No, but those are the shows I use at Cliffside. We did *Carousel*, remember? And you know I'm directing *The Mikado* this spring."

"*Carousel*, Broadway. *The Mikado*, not Broadway."

"You're splitting hairs," Augusta groused.

A knock at the door to Milly's studio interrupted them, and she ushered Elena Geller into the room.

Elena's gaze took in Milly's large studio, from the polished mahogany walls, tall windows draped in damask, to the grand piano, sitting at half-stick and graced with a Tiffany floor lamp standing next to it. The small sofa, the area rug, and chairs in one corner. Bookshelves filled with books and music. Chandelier hanging from the ceiling.

"Oh, my goodness. I took piano lessons, but my teacher's studio was in her basement. This is truly elegant, Milly."

"I feel so fortunate the Conservatory offered me this space, Elena. I love teaching here."

"Nice to see you, Elena," Augusta said. "Welcome to Milly's world."

"This is lovely, and how nice to be here with just the two of you. I have to tell you I'm uncomfortable going out in public right now. I feel like everybody is looking at me and feeling sorry for me."

Milly helped Elena with her coat and hung it on a coat rack as she replied, "I don't think that's happening, Elena." She waved toward the table.

"Well, everything is ready, so shall we partake?"

Their repast consisted of quiche Lorraine, fruit salad, roasted asparagus spears, and muffins. Augusta was impressed with the flavor and consistency and suspected the chefs in their school kitchen had been delighted for this opportunity to display their culinary expertise. The three women enjoyed the meal with only occasional small talk.

Milly cleared the dishes and served the dessert. Augusta recognized her friend's handiwork and commented, "Lemon cheesecake mousse. From the kitchen of Millicent Devereaux, I suspect."

"I didn't know you cooked, Milly," Elena said, picking up her dessert fork.

"Milly doesn't just *cook*, Elena. She's an artist in the kitchen as well as at the keyboard."

Elena's eyes closed as she took a bite of the mousse, and she sat for a moment. "Oh my goodness…that's one of the best things I've ever tasted in my life."

Augusta took a second bite of Milly's marvelous mousse…as she always thought of it. *Is it possible to get somebody drunk on food? And good, Elena's a lot more relaxed.*

"Elena, is there anything at all we can do for you?" Milly asked. "You have so much to deal with right now.

Four kids, two still in high school. All Gene's affairs to handle. I hope you have a good attorney."

"I do, and really, things aren't too overwhelming at this point." Another spoonful of mousse. "The only thing…I should do some kind of memorial service for Gene." She glanced at each of them. "We had a private…burial service. Just family and a few close friends. But Gene was really loved by so many people."

Augusta covered her mouth as she coughed. *How exactly do you mean that, Elena?*

"Indeed, he was," Milly said, kicking her friend's ankle under the table. "I know many people would like to show their support for you. And pay their respects to Gene."

"He came into contact with so many people in this city over the years," Augusta added. "And most people knew you as a couple. Didn't you get together in college?"

"Oh, yes. We met when we were freshmen at U.C. It sounds a little corny, but honestly, it was love at first sight."

Now we're getting somewhere, thought Augusta. "Everyone liked Gene. He was genuinely interested in people, and he had a certain charm that everyone responded to. Everyone back in your student days, too, I would imagine."

Elena sipped her coffee. "Well…not everyone."

"Everyone I knew," Augusta said.

"Back in our college days, though…there was this guy…he was really interested in me. Even though he knew Gene and I were together. He sometimes really made a nuisance of himself."

"How so?" asked Milly.

"Well, I ignored him as much as I could. But sometimes he'd just show up if he knew I was going to be somewhere…even if he knew Gene would be there, too."

"That's pretty bold." Augusta stirred her coffee. *Keep talking, Elena.*

"You know Gene was taking voice lessons here, and sometimes I'd come to his lessons with him. I liked doing that. I loved hearing Gene sing, and his teacher didn't mind." Elena took another spoonful of her dessert. "One day the guy showed up, and Gene was so angry, and he told him off, making a big scene. Right in this building. Downstairs in the entryway to Main Hall."

"Did he back off after that?" Augusta asked.

"He finally did. And he dropped out of U.C. not long after that happened, and moved back to Alabama, and I hoped that would be the end of it."

"And was it the end?"

Elena shifted uncomfortably in her seat. "I don't like to talk about this, but…there have been times when Gene and I hit a rough spot in our marriage."

"It happens to everybody," Augusta said reassuringly.

"So, about three years ago we were separated for several months. You may have heard that, Augusta."

"Um."

"It seems there was a friend from U.C. that Ben…that was his name…had stayed in touch with, and he found out Gene and I were apart…separated. Ben had the nerve to ask if he could see me. Oh, by then he'd moved back to Ohio and had been living in Dayton for a few years."

"And you told him to get lost," Milly said.

"Well…no…he was persistent and I was feeling neglected, so I agreed to see him."

Silence in the room for a moment. "That's understandable," Augusta commented.

"It was one of the worst mistakes I ever made. At first, he was friendly and kind and told me his wife had died, so he understood what it was to be lonely. Then he started to get aggressive and asked if we could get together. You know what I mean."

"Romantically?" Milly asked.

"Even though he was quite good-looking and had a certain charm, I never was attracted to Ben as a potential boyfriend. We had been friends, though, and I would have been okay with renewing our friendship." She gazed at each of them. "I know Gene wasn't always faithful. I guess most people know that. But he loved me, he really did. And he was always gentle and loving and kind, and he was such a great father. I tried telling that to Ben, but he became more insistent and agitated. To the point I told him to leave or I'd call the police. And I also told him I never wanted to see him or hear from him again."

"I hope that was the end of that," Augusta said. "I'm sorry that happened to you, Elena."

"I've never told this to anyone before, but I feel I have two good friends sitting here. It's a relief."

"You say he was living in Dayton at the time?" Milly asked. "I hope he moved back to Alabama."

"Sorry to say, I think he's still in Dayton. I had a letter from him after Gene's death was in the papers. He apologized for what happened the last time he saw me, and offered to help if he could. Of course, I didn't answer. Just tore up the letter and threw it out." She gazed into the distance. "It really makes me uneasy, though, knowing he's living that close."

Milly glanced at her watch. "So sorry to have to break this up, but I have a student in about a half hour and I need to contact the cafeteria staff to come up and clear all this out."

Augusta and Elena both stood. "Of course," Augusta said. "Elena, I'll walk you out."

"That's not necessary, Augusta."

"Please do let us know if we can help with plans for Gene's memorial," Augusta said, as Elena left the room.

Milly and Augusta began to collect dishes and place them in a container the cafeteria staff had provided.

"Benjamin Rodgers. Right next door in Dayton," Augusta said.

Milly stood, hands on hips. "Mal needs to know everything she told us. Rodgers might be a threat to her, Augusta."

Augusta stopped what she was doing, a stricken look on her face.

"Even worse…could he be the one who killed Gene Geller?"

Chapter 17
Yet Another Serpent

"She sounded as if she were afraid of him, Mal. The idea of him being only about an hour away isn't something she even likes to think about." Augusta gazed into his eyes.

"Odd that if he's been living there for several years, she only heard from him that one time," Mal mused. "But you said at that point, she and Geller were living apart."

"Yes, apparently someone he's stayed in touch with from their student days at U.C. told Rodgers that Elena and Gene had separated. So it must be someone who knows…knew…Gene fairly well. That's actually pretty personal information." Augusta leaned back against the sofa. "I wish I'd thought to ask if she knew who it was. Darn."

Augusta had waited until Mal returned home later that afternoon before reporting on her lunch with Milly and Elena Geller. He listened carefully to what she had to say.

189

"She received a letter from him after Eugene died," he commented. "You said she indicated it meant he was still in Dayton, so I would think that was the postmark?"

"I didn't think to ask her that. I'm not doing a very good job for you with this case, I'm afraid. But I would assume the same thing, that the letter was sent from Dayton."

Mal smiled and caressed her face. "You're doing fine. And I have enough information to make me want to learn more about Benjamin Rodgers. The Dayton PD may be able to help me with that. At least I can find out if he's been arrested for any reason."

"Do you think you need to talk to Elena again?"

"I'll have Jim do that. I don't want her to think I'm following up on your luncheon with her. She won't like being questioned again, but Jim can ask if she had seen anyone during the two times she and Gene were separated. It's a logical question since we're still drawing blanks on possible suspects."

He thought again. "Your friend at U.C. Can you contact her again and ask her to check Rodgers' records? Any extracurriculars he was involved in, any disciplinary problems? Those might be helpful."

"I'll call first thing in the morning, but she may not be in the office until Monday. I guess there's nothing that can be done this weekend."

"I need to spend some time at City Hall in the morning, and I'll give the Dayton PD a call to see if a Benjamin Rodgers is living there. I also want to pay Eloise Heinlein a visit this weekend. Nothing official, just a few questions about her encounter with Whittier. She may recall a few more details."

"With you grilling her, no doubt she will."

He grinned. "Just a friendly conversation with a nice lady who gave my wife some important information. I can do that, Gus."

Augusta was able to reach Lucy Gravetz at the University of Cincinnati the next morning.

"Do you spend your life at the University?" she laughed.

"Sometimes it feels that way. I'm here today because I'm taking Monday off for a family thing. What can I help you with?"

"The same guy, Benjamin Rodgers, class of 1945 who didn't make it to graduation. Can you check his file again and let me know about extracurricular activities, and also if there were any disciplinary problems?"

"Sure can. I'll call back in an hour or so."

Fritz curled at her feet as Augusta relaxed on the sofa, ears perked up and a quizzical expression on his face. "I know, Fritzy, and we'll go outside in a while. I want to be sure I don't miss Lucy's call." She scratched behind his ears and patted his silky head, and Fritz's tail thumped on the floor.

We talk to him just as if he were a person. Augusta chuckled. *Well, he's our guy, our doggo, part of our family.* She leaned down and hugged him, petting his flanks. *I don't like not being able to walk him; it has to be confusing that we just go out in the yard and hang around. Hopefully, this will all be over soon.*

191

Augusta thought about the young Elena Weatherly and her two suitors, Eugene Geller and Benjamin Rodgers. Despite being a devout Roman Catholic, Elena had married Gene and he had agreed their children would be raised in her faith. *But I have to believe Elena saw to it their children respected Gene's faith. Still, that may have been a strain on their marriage at times.*

Lucy called back sooner than Augusta had expected. "Extracurricular activities: pledged a fraternity, Theta Chi, as a freshman; Chess Club; no sports. There's a note here that he seemed to be one of the leaders of a rally protesting the nomination of Willard Stargel, a popular basketball and football player, the first Black student running for U.C.'s student council. And another note that Rodgers tried to start a 'secret society'…but that didn't seem to go anywhere. I do see one disciplinary action, an altercation with a fellow student who accused Rodgers of 'anti-Semitic behavior.' No particulars. One week suspension from classes. I would think it wasn't a physical altercation, or the punishment would have been more severe."

Augusta had been writing all this down as Lucy talked, but she paused. "Do you have the name of the student who made the accusation?"

"It isn't in the record. Any reason why?"

"Well, Rodgers was a rival for the affections of another student, and his rival was Jewish. I've been told the two had a confrontational relationship."

"Yes, it could certainly have been a result of that."

"No more particulars about that 'secret society'? Wonder what that was about?"

"So do I, but that was in 1943 so it's doubtful I could learn anything more."

"You're a jewel, Lucy. I owe you big time."

***

"Lieutenant Mitchell?" Eloise Heinlein's expression displayed apprehension and confusion when she opened her door.

"Miss Heinlein. I hope this isn't an inconvenient time."

"No, not at all. I assume you're here to talk about Barry Whittier." She opened the door wide and gestured for Malcolm to enter.

"This isn't an interrogation, Miss Heinlein. I thought I'd drop by and we could discuss your visit to Mr. Whittier. It's kind of you to make that effort for him."

"Eloise, please. As you know, we are admonished to visit those in prison, so I feel it's my duty. Let's go into the library, shall we? I have a fire going."

Malcolm glanced around as she ushered him down the long hallway. Everything about the house suggested money, but it was understated and tasteful. One painting he suspected might even be a French Impressionist original. *I'll have to ask Gus if she knows about that.*

The library was what he had expected, floor-to-ceiling shelves containing books. They seemed to be organized as there were many bare spaces and each shelf bore a label. A writing desk and chair, and a grouping of comfortable furniture near the fireplace.

"May I offer you coffee, Lieutenant Mitchell?" Malcolm noted the intercom near the fireplace.

"Malcolm, please. Yes, I'd appreciate that."

Eloise indicated a chair, and as Malcolm sat he continued, "As I said, I commend you on making the effort to visit your friend. How often do you see Mr. Whittier?"

"I try to go once a week. I don't mind the drive, but getting into the prison is certainly somewhat daunting." She smiled. "I've known Barry since we were children. As you know, he doesn't have many friends. I believe the result of a troubled life."

Malcolm nodded. "Since you are aware of the restrictions, you must know it's highly unlikely Mr. Whittier could reach beyond the walls and be a threat to anyone."

A maid entered with a tray and placed it on the coffee table. Eloise smiled up at her. "Thank you, Maggie."

She lifted the carafe and carefully poured coffee for each of them. "I know what Barry did was unforgivable, killing those two men. I wish I'd seen it coming and had been able to somehow keep it from happening." She stirred cream and sugar into her coffee. "You may wonder if I could have done that. I do as well. I just don't think I understood the depth of his feelings for Anton Portnov."

"Augusta and I were aware he was devastated by Portnov's death."

"Barry was a neglected child. Ignored by his father, superficially cared for by his mother when she wasn't too

194

busy with her friends and activities. She should never have had a baby. He always had nurses and governesses."

A sip of her coffee. "But he had me. We were childhood playmates. As he grew older, I began to understand how his parents' negligent attitude affected him."

She sighed. "Especially when he reached puberty. It took Barry years to accept that he was... gay...and he hated it. It had a negative effect on his entire life. But he turned that outward, too, and alienated nearly everybody he knew, one way or another."

"Yes, I understand that can happen," Malcolm said.

"Until he met Anton." Eloise gazed into her cup. "I think he really believed he might finally find some happiness. But Anton was as troubled as Barry was, and when that fell apart, I think Barry just went over the edge."

"He blamed the Chrysanthemum Quartet members for Anton's death. That was quite apparent." Malcolm helped himself to a scone.

"I never dreamed he would go to such extremes. I had urged him to see a therapist, but he refused. He said he knew what he had to do." Another sigh. "If only I had understood what he meant by that."

She sat up straighter. "So that's why I felt I should warn Augusta. I don't know what Barry could or couldn't do to her since he's incarcerated, but I saw the same look on his face I'd seen when he talked about getting even with the Quartet." *There it is*, Malcolm thought. *Something she was reluctant to say to Augusta.*

"I intend to visit the prison and speak with the authorities there to be sure they are carefully monitoring his activities," Malcolm said. "Will you continue to visit Mr. Whittier?"

"Yes, I will. Poor Barry. I wish he were getting some good therapy. And poor Anton, who I think had the same problem Barry did…refusing to accept who he was. It's rumored Anton's auto accident may have been no accident, you know. That he may have taken his own life."

"It took place out of my jurisdiction." Malcolm put down his coffee cup and stood. "Thank you for seeing me, Eloise, and filling me in about Barry Whittier's threat."

***

Augusta greeted Mal warmly, Fritz at her heels. "Did you have a productive morning?"

Mal petted the dog, who followed him into the living room. "I did. First of all, I learned a Benjamin Rodgers is living in Dayton. Monday I'll go up there and see what I can find out about the guy."

"I reached Lucy Gravetz at U.C. Not much on Rodgers' record…he joined a fraternity and was in the Chess Club." Augusta joined him on the sofa. "A one-week suspension from class after a complaint about 'anti-Semitic behavior.' An odd thing…a rumor about him being part of a group of students who wanted to establish some kind of secret society on campus. I wonder just what kind of club they hoped to start? And he was part of a rally to try to thwart the candidacy of Willard Stargel, a popular Black U.C. athlete, to student government."

"Willard Stargel? He's now head football coach at Walnut Hills High School. I've met him. A terrific guy, and a hero to the Black community."

"So...you saw Eloise?" Augusta had tucked her feet under her and turned to face him.

"Yes, I did. She reminded me she visits Whittier because it's her Christian duty, though she didn't quote chapter and verse."

"Well...did you learn anything more about her visit? You know, Mal...I do have to say her going over there can't be easy. I remember my one visit to the Workhouse when you were working on Linnea's case. What an experience. Yet Eloise continues to visit that creep Barry Whittier despite having to deal with just getting into the visitor's room." Augusta shuddered slightly. "I felt so...*invaded*...by what I had to go through."

"And you've never gone back. Eloise tries to visit Whittier every week, which requires a drive each way for nearly two hours. And even more stringent and thorough searches than you experienced before being allowed into the visitor's room. Eloise said twice that Barry has led a very troubled life. So, it's possible she is trying to be a true friend to him."

"Well, as I've often heard you say, anything is possible. On the other hand, maybe she's just bored and Barry adds a little spice to her life."

Mal laughed heartily. "Associating with a truly bad guy? I guess that could do it." He gazed at Augusta. "She does seem concerned about what Barry might be able to do, even though he's in a maximum-security prison. I'll call over to Southern Ohio State Prison on Monday and talk to the warden, just to be sure Whittier's activities are stringently monitored."

Augusta shivered slightly. "There are mafioso kingpins who have a lot of contacts on the outside. Barry Whittier doesn't fit into that category, but as Jim said, he has access to money."

She draped an arm around Mal's shoulders and kissed him warmly. "I much prefer associating with the good guys. I can't imagine my life without my cops. But I guess I should give Eloise credit for being concerned about Barry's craziness."

"Anyone who commits premeditated, cold-blooded murder isn't wired right. And that's exactly what Barry Whittier did."

They were quiet for a moment, and Mal drew Augusta close. "I have to find out who it is that wants to do you harm."

He leaned back and gazed into her eyes. "I know I'm repeating myself…but I never want to lose you."

Chapter 18
And Yet More Serpents

Monday, November 4

"Jim, can you come into my office, please?"

Spending time with his old partner while solving a case was something Mal missed. When they first worked together, Jim Edmonds was a rookie detective—now he was one of the best in the department. Mal knew Danny was in excellent hands partnering with Jim as he learned the ropes.

Mal leaned against his desk and motioned for Jim to take a seat.

"When you talk to Elena Geller today, see what you can find out about an old admirer of hers from her college days at U.C. Guy named Benjamin Rodgers, a frustrated rival of Gene Geller's. Augusta had lunch with Mrs. Geller on Friday, and learned that Rodgers contacted her a few years ago when the Gellers were separated."

"Interesting."

"From what I was told, he became aggressive and she told him to get lost. Then she had a letter from him recently after Geller's death was made public. She tore the letter up and threw it away. Augusta learned from her conversation it's possible Rodgers is living in Dayton. I'm going to talk to the DPD to see what I can find out from them."

"Do I tell Mrs. Geller we heard about him from Mrs. Mitchell?"

"I'd like to avoid that if possible. Augusta reached out to her as a friend. She first heard about Rodgers from Titus Powlett when she visited the River View Care Center. So maybe start with a phone call to him—after which he becomes an 'anonymous source.'"

"Roger that, Lieut." Jim grinned. "That will open the door for more questions about any other men she might have heard from or been in contact with since her husband's death. It seems kind of insensitive, but I think I can handle it."

"I have no doubt you can, Jim." Jim stood and both men moved toward the door.

"Say, how's Carol? And your kids? We need to get together soon."

"All doing well, thanks for asking. And let's make a definite date. Carol's talked about having you and Augusta, along with Danny and Martha, over for dinner."

"Sounds like a plan. Let's make it a potluck, why don't we?"

"Yeah, I like that idea. Especially since our wives will handle the cooking," Jim laughed.

Mal phoned Detective Andrew Keenhold, an old Marine buddy who had been with the DPD for more than twenty years, and Andy confirmed that the Benjamin Rodgers who was a resident of his city was most likely the man Malcolm was looking for.

"One arrest for shoplifting. He pleaded guilty and paid a fine. From the information we have, he's the right age for your guy. Next of kin is listed as a daughter. Rodgers has his own business, a small publishing company, which he's operated for the past eight years. Ha! Want to make a guess on what he was charged with stealing?"

"Don't tell me he pilfered a book."

"Sure did. Talk about irony. The arresting officer told me the story. Rodgers stuck it inside his jacket and waltzed out of the store. I think the price was maybe five bucks. But an employee saw him swipe it and followed him out, waving down a mall security guard. They stopped him in the parking lot. Hang on a minute."

Mal heard muffled mumbling as Andy covered the phone mouthpiece and spoke with someone.

A daughter? Gus didn't say that Elena mentioned anything about Rodgers having a daughter. She must be an adult if he used her as his next of kin.

"Sorry about that, Mal. I can't tell you much more, but if you want to come up here, we can talk to the beat cop who patrols that neighborhood."

"I can drive up right now if you have time."

"I'll make time. See you in about an hour."

Mal enjoyed the drive to Dayton, and he liked the town. He hadn't spent a lot of time there but recalled high school football games during the pre-season on a couple of occasions. His best memory was singing the Fauré *Requiem* with the Dayton Symphony. The Western Hills High School choir was one of three that were invited to participate, and he recalled the thrill of singing that great piece of music with a nearly three-hundred-voice chorus and professional soloists.

It was also good to see Andy again. They had served together in the South Pacific and became friends, and once they realized they both lived in Southern Ohio in neighboring cities, they promised to stay in touch. And they'd managed to do that, though less and less frequently as the years passed and they each had increased personal and professional responsibilities.

"Semper fi," Andy grinned as he greeted Mal. "It's been way too long."

"It sure has. We'd better make a definite date to get together before one of us assumes room temperature."

Andy laughed. "We're not *that* old, Mal. Though I see some distinguished touches of silver at your temples."

"My wife likes it, so I guess that's okay. But some of the younger detectives seem to be paying attention to me in a different way. I'm guessing they refer to me as 'the old man' when I'm out of earshot."

Andy drove them through Rodgers' neighborhood, a quiet area with older homes—Mal guessed built in the twenties or earlier—mostly two-story brick houses. Some had detached garages, some did not. Most had nicely groomed lawns; he noticed a couple with grape arbors in the back. Gardens along the sides of the house. *Much like the neighborhood where I grew up.*

"Billy Connors is meeting us at a diner a couple of streets over," Andrew said.

Connors stood when the two men joined him at a table, and Andy introduced them.

"Lieutenant Mitchell. It's an honor, sir," Connors said.

The waitress magically appeared with three coffee mugs and a carafe.

"Patrolman Connors, you've won my instant respect," Mal said with a grin.

Coffee poured, Connors said, "You want to know what I can tell you about Benjamin Rodgers. Kind of a 'problem child' in that neighborhood."

"In what way?" Mal asked, removing a pad from his inside jacket pocket and making notes.

"Nothing that could get him arrested, at least not that I've seen." Connors took a gulp of coffee. "Keeps to himself. No pets, so nothing there, and no complaints about noise. Several Jewish and immigrant families on that street, though, have gotten pamphlets in their mailboxes or stuck in their doors that suggest they'd be happier with 'their own kind' and they're not welcome in the neighborhood." He stared into his mug thoughtfully.

"It's put the whole street on edge...nobody knows who they can trust. A couple of people claim they've seen a figure late at night walking quickly up the block and onto people's porches. They think it's Rodgers, but nobody has confronted him and there's no way to prove it."

"Why do they think it could be Rodgers?"

"Some other stuff. His neighbors say he complains about Black people who come into the neighborhood for any reason. Oh, and he gets upset about young guys with long hair, too, the hippie types."

Another swallow of coffee. "And there's this…he has this great car. A Porsche, believe it or not, and the guy doesn't have a garage. So, the least little thing…maybe imaginary fingerprints, any kind of debris anywhere near the car, and he grabs me and shows me how his neighbors are disrespecting his property."

Mal let out a low whistle. "A Porsche? Why doesn't he rent a garage space for the car, since he doesn't have one? I can't imagine owning something like that and letting it sit out in the open. What color is it, by the way?"

"It's a darkish shade of blue…I think it's called 'Aetna Blue.'"

Mal lifted a brow. "You know your cars, Patrolman Connors." He made a note on the pad.

"I like cars. Maybe someday I'll even have my own Porsche." All three men chuckled.

"Lieutenant Mitchell, this has been my beat for a couple of years," Connors said. "But the beat men on the other two reliefs have been there for years and warned me about the guy. I think he's been living in his house for about seven years. I was told that at one point, Rodgers complained about a neighbor and that guy heard the conversation and threatened him. Rodgers squared off and might have laid into his neighbor if the cop hadn't been there."

A last swig of coffee. "Oh, another neighbor mentioned that Rodgers sometimes has some kind of meetings at his house. Maybe every few months. Nothing happens, except these guys creep the neighbors out. Just their attitude. They say they wouldn't be surprised to see them 'sieg heiling' each other, if you know what I mean." Connors mimicked the Nazi salute.

"Maybe KKK," Andrew commented. "We know there is such a group right here in Dayton. They stay pretty low-key, though. At least for now."

"One more thing, Patrolman Connors," Mal consulted his notes. "I understand Rodgers listed a daughter as his next of kin?"

"I've only seen her once or twice. I don't think she lives there, it seems more like she's visiting. Maybe a student, about twenty, 5'5", 120, blond, drives a Vega. Maybe a college student? She seems to be a very sweet girl. Too bad her father is such a creep."

Back at Dayton PD headquarters, Mal told Andrew why he was interested in Rodgers, finishing his story with Elena Geller reporting she was uneasy about him living so close to Cincinnati. "I'd like to get a couple of copies of his mug shot and see if anybody at Rockdale Temple remembers seeing him the day of the Avondale riot last June."

"You've got it. Tough case, Mal."

"It has been, for sure. A break would be great."

"Five copies okay? This will take about thirty minutes."

The two Marines reminisced about their time in the Pacific while they waited.

"Yeah, we definitely need to get together," Andy said, handing an envelope containing the photos to Mal.

"Thanks for these."

He turned to go, but Andy stopped him. "Mal, something I totally forgot until just now. That book Rodgers lifted? It's titled *The KKK*."

Malcolm went directly to Rockdale Temple once he returned to Cincinnati, and fortunately, most of the staff were in the building. They studied the photo carefully, but some five months had passed since June 12 and no one recalled seeing Benjamin Rodgers.

"Sorry, Lieutenant Mitchell. I wish we could be of more help," the senior rabbi said. He stared again at the photo. "Is there any chance you could leave this with me for a few days? I can show it to the members of last spring's confirmation class to see if any of them remember him."

"Excellent idea, and yes, you can hang onto it. I have more copies."

***

Mal drove to Central Parkway and turned into Frisch's Big Boy, a favorite fast-food chain in Cincinnati. He ordered a Brawny Lad steak sandwich and fries, along with a soda, and ate his quick lunch in the car. It was after one o'clock, but he wanted to make one more trip before calling it a day.

I need to drive to Lucasville to see Barry Whittier and talk to him...to make it very clear that if he tries anything, anything at all, with my wife, there'll be hell to pay. He may already be in prison for life, but he's not in solitary. And he wouldn't like that—a freak show like Whittier needs to be able to strut his stuff to hang onto whatever sanity he has left.

He stopped at a pay phone and called the warden to set up the meeting, then phoned Detective HQ and talked to Jim Edmonds, senior of the detectives on duty.

"Do I need to get back to the office, or is everything copacetic?"

"Nothing we can't handle, Mal. A pretty quiet day."

"Good, then I have one more thing I want to do which will take the rest of the afternoon. Are you picking up Augusta at the Conservatory?"

"Yes, I am."

"Please tell her I may not be home until after six. She doesn't need to know why, but you do. I'm going to drive over to Lucasville if you need to reach me."

"To talk to Whittier?"

"Just want to set him straight. Thanks, Jim."

Chapter 19
The Second of Three Trials

Mal arrived home to find Milly's car in the driveway, and Garrett and Milly inside unpacking the dinner they had brought for him and Augusta.

"We won't stay, Mal," Garrett said. "Milly just wanted to be sure you guys are doing okay, so she prepared dinner with you in mind. She knows you like Mediterranean food."

"You know you're always welcome," Mal responded, but Augusta caught the slight hesitation in his voice. Garrett was aware of the situation, and they didn't linger.

After Malcolm and Augusta finished Milly's delicious meal of moussaka, Greek salad, crusty bread, and baklava, and cleaned up the kitchen, Augusta went upstairs. Malcolm took Fritz for a walk before joining her.

"It was all right to let them come over, wasn't it?" She lay on the chaise in a soft robe and slippers.

"This once. I need to know if anyone wants to come to the house, though." Mal placed his gun and holster on top of the chiffonier and hung up his jacket, then perched on the edge of the chaise and kissed her.

"Did you have a productive day? I was a little surprised you didn't get home until so late."

"After I went to Dayton, I went to see Barry Whittier," he replied. He felt her grow tense as he held her.

"Sorry to say, Eloise Heinlein was right. Whittier seems to have developed a major case of blaming you for his troubles," Mal reported. "No matter how firmly I said he was responsible for his misdeeds, for some reason he's twisted all this in his head. He's always blamed the Chrysanthemum Quartet members for Anton Portnov's suicide, and now he's worked you into the mix for that as well."

Augusta shivered slightly. "So it's very possible he was responsible for cutting my brake cable."

"Possible, but not likely. The warden assured me Whittier is watched carefully, and any phone calls and visits are closely monitored. The warden reads his mail, whether incoming or outgoing, and hasn't seen anything suspicious. Whittier has very few visitors, mostly just Eloise, and seldom receives or makes a phone call. Prisoners have to ask permission to use the phone and are limited in the amount of time they can talk. There are guards everywhere."

"What about access to his money?" Augusta asked

Mal stood and unbuttoned his shirt. "Well, we know he has funds, but at this point, I doubt he's able to get his hands on them."

"But you don't know that for a fact."

"No, I don't. But I honestly don't think he had anything to do with your automobile incident, Gus."

"Then who could it have been? I hate to think it might have been a student." Augusta turned down the duvet and they both climbed into bed.

Mal leaned on an elbow. "I understand that. But maybe someone connected to a student? A family member, a friend…someone who has a strong objection to how you've cast this opera."

"I guess anything is possible, Mal."

She moved close to him, and he took her in his arms.

"How much longer am I going to be under house arrest? I need to get to Cliffside for my lessons, and I want my car back."

"You know I can't answer that, and your car is still at the lab." He paused. "Here's what I need you to do. Tomorrow morning, since Sister Mary Norbert is still substituting for you with your students at Cliffside, I need you to carefully go through your cast list. Mark any that you think might have the slightest bit of anger about not getting the major roles in which you cast the Black and Japanese American singers. Also, if you are aware of where these people come from, mark any from the south."

"Oh, I know where most of them are from. That won't be a problem. You're thinking some of those students might have relatives who are strongly prejudiced against any ethnicity other than white? While I hate the idea, I've wondered about that myself. But even if some people don't like it, many of the best singers and musicians have always been of other races."

"Something I heard today…and I'd heard it before… there may be a branch of the Ku Klux Klan in southern Ohio, in or near Dayton. Though I don't know what the connection could be between that group and a student opera production in Cincinnati."

"Mal, speaking of your visit to Dayton today, did you learn anything valuable about Benjamin Rodgers that keeps him on the list of suspects for Gene Geller's death?"

"I don't want to say too much, but yes, I did. Enough to make me want to dig deeper. I can tell you he is without a doubt a bigot, even possibly a member of the KKK."

"All of this is…." Augusta waved a hand. "I can't even come up with a word. What's the *matter* with people? Live and let live. Even better, value people for the colors in their character, not the color of their skin…to paraphrase Dr. Martin Luther King."

Mal kissed her. "Well said, my beautiful bride."

***

Augusta stopped at Milly's studio before heading for her own. "Miriam called me just before I left my house. She has the flu and can't play tonight. Any chance you could substitute?"

"Sure can. What time do you want me there? I need to run home if I have time."

"The cast is called for six-thirty. I like to be there half an hour earlier."

"I'll be there before six-thirty, no problem. Just need a score."

Augusta reached into her bag. "And presto! Just like magic, you have one," she laughed.

"What are we doing tonight?" Milly flipped through the score.

"Working on the ensembles. Hopefully, the two female trios will have spent time on their own and we'll get through those pieces quickly. Some are a bit more complicated, as you know."

"I should say. I know some of the arias are showstoppers, but the ensembles are where this opera shines. Such a variety of musical styles...even of musical eras."

"Two of my favorites are the quintet with the Three Ladies, Tamino, and Papageno. And the trio with Tamino, Pamina, and Sarastro. Thanks a million for agreeing to play."

"I'll enjoy it." Milly paused, closing the score and hugging it to her chest. "You know, I had the feeling Malcolm wasn't too thrilled to see us at your house last night."

"After you left, he told me he'd prefer to know in advance if anyone is coming to visit. Until we find out who tampered with my brakes."

"That makes sense."

"Not only are we limiting visitors, but I haven't been permitted to go to Cliffside since the incident. Thank heavens for Sister Norbert, she's holding down the fort for me until I get back."

Augusta's one Tuesday afternoon student had canceled, but she had come in well before the rehearsal to spend some time looking through the music scheduled to be rehearsed. She planned to grab a quick supper in the school cafeteria.

She opened her score and turned to the first act finale. *This is where we begin to learn the truth*, Augusta thought. *When we meet Sarastro. He eventually sets Tamino's feet on the right path.*

Interesting concept…'setting someone's feet on the right path.' Think how serene the world would be if that happened more often than not, rather than people following organizations like the KKK.

A tap on her door and Augusta opened it to see Allan Meissner. "Do you have a few minutes, Professor McKee?"

"Allan, any man who has been to hell and back in Vietnam can certainly be considered as much a friend as a student. Please call me Augusta, at least when it's just us."

"Thank you." He sank into the upholstered chair opposite her desk, stretching out his long legs. "That's kind of what I wanted to talk to you about."

"Your time in Vietnam?"

"You may be aware of this. One of our greatest problems over there is we can't always tell friend from foe. I really get the message that's in this opera."

"I'd heard that before. There was a major battle at a base because of that, if I'm not mistaken."

"You're not mistaken. Marble Mountain, near Da Nang. I was there when the base was attacked by the Viet Cong, and some of the Vietnamese who were working on the base joined them."

Allan stretched out his hands and stared at his long fingers. "What I've had to do with these hands...I don't like to think about it. I never talk about it."

Augusta walked around to the front of her desk and placed her hands on his shoulders. "Allan, you can talk to me about anything. I mean that."

She saw the tears that sprang into his eyes. "Coming home...it hasn't been easy."

"I'm sure it hasn't, with all the upheaval in this country," She gazed into his face. "Use your music, Allan. The music that is so much a part of you. Open yourself up to it and I honestly believe it will help you heal."

A faint smile. "That's what I'm trying to do. And it is helping. Singing this character...I can't tell you how much it means to have this wonderful music to perform. Sarastro is all about the good in the universe. I really needed him."

This is enough, thought Augusta. *If performing in this opera helps this deeply troubled young man find his way back, it makes everything worthwhile.*

***

The six women who were playing the Queen's Ladies and the Three Spirits had evidently spent time on their own rehearsing the music, and Byron Matthias was pleased with what he heard. He glanced around and asked Augusta, "Where's Tamino?'

"George will be here around seven-thirty. He had an engagement to sing for a women's organization before a dinner."

Byron nodded. "We'll come back to the quintet and trio when he gets here."

George came in just as they were working through the first act finale, after which Byron gave them a short break. Augusta was pleased when she saw George sit down next to Allan and strike up a conversation, and even more pleased when Allan responded. *Talking about music, no doubt*, she thought. *Let's hope a friendship grows from this. George is a good person, and he's also a charmer.*

The rehearsal resumed with the quintet Augusta had mentioned to Milly, which required working out some sections more carefully. They managed to run through the second act finale, which would need more work, but Byron dismissed the cast promptly at nine.

Augusta knew Jim and Dan, who were her ride home, had been keeping an eye on the school for more than three hours. While she was again thanking Milly for covering for the pianist, George joined them.

"Professor Devereaux, was someone using your car tonight?"

Startled, Milly replied, "Good heavens, no. Why do you ask?"

"Well, I parked near it and I saw someone, a man I think, standing next to it, in the shadows. It looked as if he might have been doing something…it seemed odd, so I thought I should say something."

Forcing herself to ignore the shiver that ran up her spine, Augusta said, "Both of you, come with me." *Now what?* She found Danny and Jim near the side entrance to Main Hall and asked George to repeat what he had told Milly.

Jim immediately went on high alert. "Where's the car? I need make, model, license number, and your keys."

"All of you, stay here," Danny said, and the two detectives strode outside.

Waiting seemed to take an eternity, and it was impossible to attempt small talk. Quivering inside, Augusta put an arm around Milly's waist. She'd seldom seen her friend at a complete loss for words. Less than half an hour later Danny returned.

"Jim's waiting for a tow for your car, Milly. George, you probably saved Professor Devereaux's life." No one said anything for a few moments.

"But why would someone cut Milly's brake cable?" Augusta finally asked.

"It's worse than that. There was an explosive device under the hood. Fortunately, Jim is trained in explosives and found it and disarmed it quickly. It would have gone off the minute Milly turned the key in the ignition."

"Good Lord, Dan," Milly gasped out. "Are you serious?"

"Yes, I am. Lieutenant Mitchell should be here at any minute, and he'll let you know what happens next."

Malcolm had in fact arrived on the scene and now came inside Main Hall. "I'm taking both of you ladies home," he announced. "George, we can't thank you enough for being observant and letting Professor Devereaux know about the possibility her car was tampered with. Did you observe anything about the man that might help us identify him?"

"No, sir…sorry. He was just a shape in the shadows."

"We may need to talk with you again, but for now, you're free to leave. And do not mention this incident to anyone."

"Roger that, Lieutenant Mitchell," George said, proud to use a little "cop talk."

Milly hugged George and they said their goodnights, Milly thanking him profusely. Augusta turned to Mal and repeated what she had said earlier. "Why on earth would someone want to harm Milly?"

Since Mal was now on duty, Augusta had to sit with Milly in the back seat. He opened the door for them and they slid into the car.

"Jim tells me you went outside before the rehearsal tonight," Mal told Augusta, looking over the seat to talk.

"I just ran down to Milly's car to get her score. I'm sorry, Mal. Jim was coming down the driveway to get me when I came back."

"It's possible the person who booby-trapped Milly's car saw you and thought that was the car you'd be leaving in, because he couldn't find yours. We don't know that you were the intended target, but it's likely that was the case. I'm putting a detail on both of you round the clock. Milly, I'll take you home first. You'll need to pack a bag and stay with us."

Milly clutched her arm, and Augusta couldn't stop the strong chill that ran through her.

"So, since it doesn't appear to be Barry Whittier, who would do these horrible things?"

Chapter 20
The Truth Begins to Dawn

"Is Stoddard at your place?" Mal asked Milly, as they headed for her house.

"He should be."

"Garrett is welcome to stay with us as well until we get this mess resolved," Mal told her.

"I understand," Milly said, visibly shaken.

"Another thing. Neither you nor Augusta is to leave the house unless a detective is with you. That means canceling all your activities for the present." He looked at his wife in the rear-view mirror, adjusting it so it was clear he was talking to her. "Understood?"

"Yes, understood," Augusta replied meekly. *Mal is really angry with me,* she thought. *And with good reason.*

Once everyone was back at Augusta and Malcolm's and the relief detail had arrived, Mal spoke briefly with Jim and Danny.

"Back to the Geller case—I left the mug shot of Rodgers at Rockdale Temple, and by now the head rabbi may have shown it to members of the confirmation class who were at the Temple on June twelfth. I need the two of you to check back with him and if any of those young people recognized Rodgers, bring them into headquarters to interview them. Find out what happened that made them remember seeing him."

"Copy that," Jim replied.

After Jim and Danny left, Mal headed upstairs to find a distraught Augusta sitting on the bed wrapped in a blanket.

"Mal, I can't believe how careless it was for me to leave the Conservatory unaccompanied. And because of my stupidity, I put Milly's life in danger. I'll never forgive myself for that."

"Your young tenor saved the day. Milly's car being tampered with during a rehearsal with you convinces me that you were the intended target. We need to seriously investigate the possibility that these attacks are from a member of your cast—or a member who has a relative or friend with a possible affiliation with the KKK or some other hate group. They can wreak all sorts of havoc."

"All I did was make sure every student in the Conservatory had an equal opportunity when we cast the opera."

"The kind of thing those groups abhor. Fortunately, nobody was hurt tonight. But you and Milly must follow instructions at this point, Augusta." He pulled her into his arms. "I promise you I will take down this S.O.B. as quickly as possible."

***

The atmosphere in the McKee-Mitchell home was subdued the next morning. Milly and Augusta prepared breakfast for the four of them, which was eaten mostly in silence. Mal left immediately to go to Headquarters.

Garrett gazed out the front window and eyed the new unmarked police car. "Well, your 'minders' are here for the day, I guess," he commented. "As for me, I'm due at my office." He gave Milly a quick kiss and headed out the door.

"This feels so weird. I know a cop car followed us to River View Care Center…but this is totally different." Milly wiped down the table vigorously. "So, Augusta, what do we do for the rest of the day?"

"Good question. Mal already walked Fritz and said he'd be home for lunch and to take him out again. I hate that I can't at least do that." They wandered into the living room and sank into the sofa, Fritz at Augusta's heels.

"Milly, I'm so sorry I got you into this. If I had followed Mal's orders, this wouldn't have happened and you wouldn't be stuck here."

"You just hush, Augusta. If the bastard hadn't done that, he'd have done something else…and maybe he would have succeeded. Thank goodness for George Van Dorn."

"Yes, thank goodness for George."

"And besides, if you always followed orders, you wouldn't be our Augusta McKee."

Augusta managed a wan smile, and they sat silently for a moment or two.

"Well, we can't just sit here and stare at each other." Milly slapped her knees and stood. "Let's make some music."

She sat at the piano and played a few measures of Chopin's "Fantaisie-Impromptu."

"Oh, don't stop. I love hearing you play that." Augusta patted Fritz's head as Milly's skilled fingers brought Chopin's beautiful music to life.

"Fabulous," Augusta sighed. "You're right, making music is a great idea."

She went to the shelves behind the piano and began removing a few books of vocal solos.

"When was the last time you gave a recital, anyway?" Milly glanced over the first song Augusta handed her, a Schubert song both women particularly loved.

"Maybe three years? You know what? Why don't we plan a joint recital for some time in the spring?"

"Let's do that. It'll be fun."

Time passed quickly as they engrossed themselves in their art. Augusta put music in front of Milly, songs by Schumann, Schubert, Duparc, and Fauré. Milly played through them, and Augusta began to sing bits and pieces. "I didn't warm up."

"You sound pretty damn good to me," Milly picked up another book and peered at it. "I don't think I've ever heard you sing Rachmaninoff."

"I don't. I think it's better suited to a male voice."

"Except for this one," Milly opened to the "Vocalise." "Perfect for soprano."

"Also bloody hard to sing," Augusta remarked, but Milly had already begun the introduction, and Augusta couldn't resist attempting it.

Soon she was caught up in the beauty and poignancy of the music, and the two women continued through the drama of the entire piece, bringing it to a quiet close. Augusta touched her face and was surprised to find tears. She didn't realize how emotional she had become.

She and Milly also hadn't heard Mal and Garrett come into the house, and it startled Augusta to hear Mal say, "I've never heard you sing that. What a beautiful piece."

"Not sung as well as it deserves, I'm afraid. That high C-sharp wasn't great."

Milly relieved Garrett of the bags of food he had brought in. "Oh, lunch from Meck's. You men are the best."

The two of them went into the kitchen to prepare plates for lunch, and Mal kissed Augusta warmly. "What a treat to come into the house and hear you singing. You don't do it nearly often enough."

She leaned back and examined his face. "I think you've made some progress with your case. But which one?"

"Let's have lunch and I can tell all of you some of what I've learned."

"Is Garrett involved in this in some way?"

"He was in City Hall and stopped by Detective Headquarters to see if I wanted to have lunch. We decided to pick it up and bring it back here. I know how difficult this is for you, and for Milly as well."

Seated in the alcove, Mal told them he'd heard from the rabbi at Rockdale Temple. "Three of the confirmation class members who were at the Temple on June twelfth positively identified Benjamin Rodgers. They recalled seeing him when they were trying to get away from the Temple that day. They're coming in this afternoon so Jim and Dan can interview them. We need to know what makes them so sure they saw him."

"Elena Geller may have been right to be uneasy about Rodgers living so close by," Augusta said. She paused. "You believe he may have killed Gene."

"He's a viable suspect. We have to consider he may attempt to approach Elena again, but Jim found out when he spoke with her that Amanda and her kids are presently staying with Elena and her family. We may need to talk to her again, but I think for now she's safe and has some protection."

He leaned back. "I've learned some things about Rodgers. For one thing, it's likely he's associated with the KKK."

"Making bigotry another motive for killing Geller," interjected Garrett.

Mal nodded. "Rodgers is intensely disliked in the neighborhood. His neighbors are convinced the mysterious pamphlets that appear in their doors and mailboxes suggesting they move out are hate mail from Rodgers." Mal took a gulp of his soft drink. "Most of his neighbors are Jewish. Some are immigrants."

"What kind of sick thing is that for a man to do?" Augusta was horrified.

"You have a picture of Rodgers with you?" Garrett asked.

Mal produced one and laid it on the table. Augusta picked it up and studied it. *Mug shots are pretty unflattering, but he's not a bad-looking man. Blond, blue-eyed. Maybe a poster boy for the KKK?*

"You mentioned the KKK," Milly said. "Isn't that group pretty much defunct? Wasn't it a result of all the problems with Reconstruction, and terrorizing the former slave population in the South?"

"People who hate will always find a way to organize and try to spread the hate," Garrett said. "The Ku Klux Klan has appeared in this country in three waves…the first was during Reconstruction, but that eventually died out. Then they were resurrected around the time of the First World War, bigger and better than ever. At one time it was estimated there may have been eight million members."

Milly shivered. "Good Lord. I had no idea. That's scary."

Garrett continued, "Pearl Harbor pretty much put an end to the organization until after World War II. People had better things to do and think about. But eventually, they started to rebuild, only on a much smaller scale. These days the KKK is targeting anybody who isn't white and protestant. No, Anglo-Saxon, white, and protestant. Oh, and heterosexual. The Civil Rights Movement has fanned their hatred and their violent activity. And they must be stirred up by the Avondale riot."

"Hate is an interesting concept," Mal commented. "Personally, I've never understood it."

"Yet as a law enforcement officer, you deal with it constantly," Garrett said.

Mal pushed his chair back and stood. "I have to get back to HQ, and I'm sure I don't have to remind any of you to keep this information to yourselves."

"I'm the volunteer Fritz-walker for the moment," Garrett said, also standing. "C'mon, dog."

Augusta and Milly stared at each other once the men had left.

"Milly…what kind of world are we living in these days?"

"We've talked about this before. One we have a difficult time understanding." She ran a hand over her springy curls. "I'll clean up, and then do you mind if I practice? It helps me deal with everything better."

"Oh, Mal forgot the photo of Rodgers," Augusta picked it up and again looked at it. "Practice? Be my guest. I have something I need to check on. I'll be upstairs if you need me, and thanks for doing K.P. duty."

Augusta had a room in her house which was entirely hers. A full-length mirror covered half the interior wall, reflecting a small ballet barre that she used daily. Bookshelves and a desk and chair were situated near the window.

Going to her desk, Augusta pulled a paper from her briefcase and sat down to study it. It was the full cast list for *The Magic Flute*.

She placed another sheet of paper next to it and removed a sharpened pencil from the desk drawer.

Thirty-three names. She studied each carefully, envisioning each cast member as she did so. The principals were listed at the top. The Queen of the Night, Pamina, Papagena, Tamino, Sarastro, Papageno, Monostatos. She knew each of those performers well and two were also her private students, George Van Dorn and Denise James. None of these were names she had provided to Mal as having family in the south. There had been eight such names, three were sophomores, and the other five upperclassmen. *But someone....*

Next on her list, the Queen's Three Ladies. First Lady...Gloria Gardner.

Augusta sat up straighter. *Sweet girl, lovely voice. Blond, blue-eyed sophomore, private voice teacher is Professor Claudia Prince. Friendly with Denise and George, I often see them together at lunch and chatting during rehearsal breaks. In fact, the three of them came in together last night.*

Gloria Gardner. Augusta had dropped the photo Mal left behind on her desk, and picked it up again. *Around the eyes...and the chin...and I hear what could be a hint of a southern accent sometimes when she speaks. But Elena never said anything about Rodgers having a daughter and neither did Mal...and why the different last name?*

Augusta swiftly took the few steps to her bedroom and telephoned the Conservatory, asking to be connected to the office. *I remember Gloria's place of residence when I checked was listed as Ohio.* A flutter in her chest. *Not from the south, but....*

The dean's secretary took her call. "Alice, it's Augusta McKee. I'm checking on a few things about cast members for *The Magic Flute*, and I don't seem to have the name of Gloria Gardner's high school for the program." *Oh, I lie so easily when I'm doing this,* Augusta thought, biting back the giggle she felt rising in her throat.

"Sure, I can get that for you, Augusta. If you can hold, I'll look it up right now."

"You're the best, Alice."

Augusta glanced out the window at a gray day, growing gloomier by the minute. Rain had been predicted for this afternoon and the day seemed ready to fulfill the prophecy.

"Here it is. Sidney Lanier High School."

"Sidney Lanier High School? Named for the famous southern poet?"

"Yes, it's in Montgomery, Alabama."

"Got it. Thanks so much."

Augusta sat for a moment, still holding the handset after she'd returned it to the phone. *Sidney Lanier High School. Famous southern poet. Montgomery, Alabama. I'm sure Gloria's application claimed residence in Ohio…Dayton, in fact. I remember that now.*

Could Gloria Gardner be Benjamin Rodgers' daughter?

Benjamin Rodgers is a racist.

It's likely Benjamin Rodgers killed Eugene Geller… and now he could be trying to kill me.

Chapter 21
More of the Truth Comes to Light

A clap of thunder pulled Augusta from her reverie, and she was aware of Milly playing, but didn't recognize the piece...she thought it might be Rachmaninoff.

She moved to the window. Seeing the unmarked car in front of her house now gave her a feeling of being protected rather than being confined. *Interesting how quickly our perspective can change*, she thought, watching the rain begin to fall.

Augusta didn't think she had enough to contact Mal yet with her suspicions about Benjamin Rodgers. *And I can't talk to George Van Dorn. He'll immediately suspect something bizarre and want to play cop.* She made another call to the Conservatory.

"This is Augusta McKee. Is Professor Prince available? I don't want to interrupt a lesson," she told the student operator.

"Sorry you're under the weather, Professor McKee. Please hold and I'll check her schedule." A different student from the one she had spoken to earlier that morning when she requested a note be placed on her door, informing her students that due to illness she wouldn't be teaching.

"Claudia Prince."

"Claudia, it's Augusta. I hope I'm not interrupting a lesson." Augusta wound the cord to the handset around her hand.

"Not at all. My student canceled. Maybe she has the same bug you're dealing with. Sorry you're ill."

"I'm sure I'll be fine in a day or two," Augusta lied. "Actually, I've been considering assigning understudies to some of the leading roles in *The Magic Flute*, and I wanted to talk to you about Gloria Gardner. I'm impressed with her."

"She's a gem," Claudia responded. "Unusually fine natural voice, terrific work ethic. Quick study."

"Just curious…I noticed she has Dayton as her home address but she graduated from a high school in Montgomery. Did she move recently?"

"Interesting story about Gloria. From what she's told me, her parents split up when she was quite young … she was only five or six, I think. Her mother never remarried, so they lived with her mother's parents. Sadly, during her senior year of high school, Gloria's mother died of cancer. Her father had moved to Dayton at some point and Gloria visited him occasionally. He suggested she move to Dayton after her mother's death."

"So she lives with him now?"

"Well…not really. She stayed with him the summer before she entered school here, but these days she seldom leaves Cincinnati. She hasn't said much about her father; she's very reserved when I ask about him."

"How so?"

"I don't pry, but some of my students love talking about how supportive their parents are and how much their family means to them."

"Yes, I hear that as well," Augusta commented.

"Gloria usually gives me brief answers if I ask about her dad and then changes the subject. I have a feeling she visits him out of a sense of duty and not because she likes spending time with him."

"She doesn't go to his house over the holidays?"

"She goes back to Montgomery to be with her grandparents. And I don't know this for a fact, but I believe the grandparents are responsible for her tuition and other expenses."

Who can tell me if her father's last name is different? Darn. I may have to talk to George after all.

"Are you thinking of her as an understudy for Pamina?"

"Yes, I am," Augusta said, lying again. "I haven't definitely decided to do this, but she's one of two girls I had in mind. Anything else about her that I should know?"

A tap on her door and Milly stuck her head in. Augusta lifted a hand with one finger up, asking for one more minute.

"You may have noticed that Gloria is well-liked. She's genuinely thrilled with her role. I recall she was very excited for her friend Denise when you announced the cast."

"That's great to hear. Thanks again." Augusta cradled the handset.

Milly lifted an eyebrow. "And that was…?"

"Claudia Prince. Sorry, Mil, but I need to make one more call, and then I'll come downstairs and talk to you."

"Rachmaninoff and Debussy await." Milly closed the door and Augusta heard her humming as she headed back downstairs, Fritz right behind her. *I guess Fritzer likes Rachmaninoff*, Augusta thought.

Before Augusta could place her call to Malcolm, the phone rang, and it was Dennis Halloran.

"Augusta, are you ill? Sister Norbert told me she's been holding down the fort for you for nearly a week."

"No, I'm…fine. At least, I'm not ill." *How much can I tell him? Of all the people I know, Dennis can best keep a confidence. His priestly duties demand it.*

"Dennis, I can't say too much, but at present I'm being guarded by a round-the-clock police detail. Needless to say, that's curtailed my activities."

"Good Lord, Augusta! What happened?"

"Well, last Tuesday my brakes failed when I started driving home from a rehearsal. Oh, before that…I had three anonymous notes that were threatening. Of course, the detectives are working to learn who seems to want me…," her voice trailed off. *I can't say it.*

"Threatening notes? Some kind of hate mail?" His voice grew sharp. "Were your brakes deliberately disabled?"

"It appears that they were." Augusta hooked her elbow over the headboard and adjusted the handset. "And then last night someone placed an explosive device in Milly's car while we were at rehearsal, apparently thinking she would be driving me home. The police disabled the device and no one was hurt."

"Dear God, Augusta!"

"I know you and I talked about the possibility of some people not being too thrilled with me casting an ethnically diverse opera, but who could have ever dreamed this would happen?"

"I don't suppose there's a thing I can do other than continue to pray for you." He paused. "And for the person...or people...who've attacked you."

"Yes, I suppose you're obligated to do that. You'll forgive me if I can't follow your good example."

"Not my example. The Master I follow set the example, Augusta, when he was put to death unjustly. Loving and forgiving those who wronged him." He sighed. "I didn't mean to preach. Please tell me if there is anything at all I can do."

"You're doing it, Dennis. I'll let you know what happens."

"God bless you, my dear friend and sister."

"Thank you, Father Halloran."

Augusta felt tears gathering in her throat and had to collect herself before calling Malcolm. *Dennis is the consummate Jesuit,* she thought. *Seeing and loving God in all things, and all people. Even people like Barry Whittier and Benjamin Rodgers.*

Malcolm answered her call immediately, and she told him everything she had learned about Gloria Gardner, including her resemblance to Rodgers.

After a short silence, Mal responded, "As a matter of fact, Benjamin Rodgers *does* have a daughter. The beat cop I talked to even described her as blonde, about five-five, trim. He said she seemed to be a very nice girl. He also said she doesn't spend much time at Rodgers' house."

"Well, after what you told us at lunch about his possible involvement with the KKK, I've had a bad feeling about him. About whether he might be the same person who's...." she broke off, again unable to say it. *The person who is trying to kill me. The person who wants me dead.*

"This is important information, Gus. Huge, in fact. Identifying our prime suspect in the Geller murder as the same person trying to kill you would be the big break in the case...both cases. But Gus, it has to be hard for you to put a face to the person who has you targeted."

"I have to admit it's a shock. But now I'm trying to think how I can find out for sure if Gloria Gardner is Rodgers' daughter. I could talk to George, but I'm reluctant to involve him and I'm not even sure what to ask him."

"There may be a fairly easy way. Rodgers' daughter has a car, and you tell me Gloria Gardner occasionally visits her father in Dayton. If they are the same girl, I would think she might very well have an Ohio driver's license on file with the Bureau of Motor Vehicles."

"Well, you have her name, and you know Rodgers' address. Can you find that out for us, Lieutenant Mitchell?"

"You bet. I'll call you back, this shouldn't take much time. You have great instincts, Gus. I have a gut feeling you're right about this." A pause. "Are you okay?"

"I will be," she said. "And Mal, this sure puts a whole different light on the two detectives sitting in my driveway. It's gone from being 'under house arrest' to being 'in protective custody' in a heartbeat. I can't thank you enough for that."

A quiet chuckle. "Glad you're hanging onto your sense of humor, bride."

"Mal, can I tell Milly any of this? After all…she almost became collateral damage."

"Yes, I don't see any harm in you letting her know what you've learned. Just sit tight for the moment. I'll get back to you after I've checked on the driver's license."

Once downstairs, Augusta headed for the kitchen, motioning Milly to follow her.

"This is going to require ice cream," she said. "Large bowls. Mint chocolate chip or peanut butter ripple?"

Mal called back not long after Augusta filled Milly in on what she had just learned.

"Gloria Gardner has an Ohio license, and the address is the same as Benjamin Rodgers'. She has to be his daughter."

"Well, that only proves that Rodgers could be the person angry with the way I cast *The Magic Flute*…his daughter being passed over for a leading role for a Black soprano. George Van Dorn may know more about

Gloria, since they seem to be quite friendly. I told you why I didn't think it was a good idea for me to be the person to talk with him. He thinks we're best buddies."

"Understandably," Mal chuckled. "You did have quite an adventure together when he was kidnapped. I'll have him come down here for a talk and let you know what I find out."

"Well, George could be helpful in learning more about Benjamin Rodgers, but that won't be much help in confirming him as Eugene Geller's murderer, will it?" Sitting in the alcove, Augusta watched the rain coming down steadily. *Not my favorite kind of weather.*

"I'm waiting to hear from Jim and Dan about what the Rockdale Temple confirmation candidates from last spring have to say."

Augusta turned to Milly after she hung up the phone. "I guess you heard. Gloria Gardner is Benjamin Rodgers' daughter. At present, Jim and Dan are waiting for the three teens from Rockdale so they can be interviewed."

"And I gather Malcolm is going to have George come in so he can talk to him. Sounds like a plan."

Augusta stared at her now-empty ice cream bowl. "I never even thought about Gloria being related to this man I'd heard about from Titus Powlett."

"Why would you, when she's using another name? It's possible she used her father's address when she applied to the Conservatory, thinking she might move up here. It would be a way to pay a little less in tuition," Milly commented.

Fritz lay near the wall, tail thumping, looking from one woman to the other.

"Don't tell Mal I did this," Augusta said as she set her bowl on the floor for Fritz to lick. He eagerly dashed to the bowl, licking it clean with three or four swipes of his tongue, causing both women to laugh.

"I guess he seldom gets a taste of ice cream," Milly chortled. "But my goodness, does he ever love it."

Augusta glanced at the window. "It's stopped raining. I should let him out into the yard for a bit. I need to wave at our bodyguards to let them know I'm going to do that." She went to the front door and gave the two detectives on duty a hand wave.

One left the car and walked around to the back while Fritz was in the yard with her. He circled the house, checking up and down the street.

"Do you know these detectives?" Milly asked.

"Not really. I've met them. All of them are terrific people in my book. Jim and Danny will be on duty tonight." She called to Fritz to come inside, and he obediently returned to the house, tail wagging.

"He doesn't bark much, does he?" Milly said.

"He's been well trained, but no, he was never much of a barker. Let's face it, he gets everything he needs without having to raise a ruckus." She petted her dog. "Look at us, Milly, fussing over Fritz in the midst of a crisis."

"Better than worrying over a crisis we can't do much about, don't you agree? Pretty observant of you, though, to realize Gloria might be related to Benjamin Rodgers. I'm sure that was a huge help to the detectives."

239

Mal telephoned again to update Augusta. "The teens who recognized Rodgers were interviewed separately, and they had pretty much the same story to tell," he said. "When Geller was ushering the kids out of the Temple during the riot, the man in the photo came pushing up through the crowd from behind and almost knocked one of the boys down. It looked like he was trying to catch up to Geller, but then he dropped back and none of them saw him again. They assumed he was the dad of one of the kids and they all agreed Geller never saw him. In all the chaos and confusion, they'd forgotten this happened, and didn't remember the man when we questioned them after Geller's disappearance or again after the murder was discovered. Not until we showed them Rodgers' mug shot."

"And they were all sure the man they saw was Rodgers?"

"Positive."

"So he was at the scene and likely is your killer," Augusta said.

"I'm waiting to interview George, and then I'll talk to my Marine buddy in Dayton. I have some questions for the beat cops on Rodgers' street."

"Such as?"

"Such as, was his car in its usual parking spot last night?"

"Because if not, it means he could have been in Cincinnati last night," Augusta said. "Putting an explosive device in Milly's car."

It could. Unless something else comes up, I should be home by six or so. Everything okay there?"

"Yes, fine. Do you think you have enough to pick Rodgers up?"

"We're getting close," Malcolm responded. "I need to hear what George has to say about Rodgers' relationship with his daughter. We may get some valuable information from him. Talk to you later."

Milly grew thoughtful as she heard this new information.

"I'm concerned about Elena. Regardless of her sister 'Annie Oakley' being there with her, maybe she needs protection, too. Rodgers is behaving so erratically he might very well attempt to see her again." She sighed. "What I don't get is how he went from being a bigot and a would-be homewrecker only a few years ago to a cold-blooded killer at this point. What is this guy...a psychopath?"

Augusta took a deep breath as she felt a flutter in her stomach.

"You may have just hit the nail on the head." She stood and went to the window as rain began falling again.

"And if that's the case...who knows what he might try next?"

Susan Moore Jordan

Chapter 22
The Third Trial

George carefully studied the photo Mal had handed him. "I can't say if it was this man or not. The light was dim, and I was across the street. Sorry, Lieutenant Mitchell."

"That's fine, George. I appreciate your coming in to take a look at the picture." He reached across his desk as George returned the mug shot of Benjamin Rodgers to him.

"Before you go, George, I'd like to ask you about something, and please understand this conversation is confidential and I need you not to speak about it with anyone."

"Sure, Lieutenant Mitchell." George sat forward.

"I hear from my wife that you are friends with Gloria Gardner. Does she talk about her father with you at all?"

George's eyes widened. "Sometimes she does, as a matter of act. She visits him in Dayton once in a while, and two or three times he's showed up in Cincinnati to take her to dinner. It's kinda sad...I don't think she gets along with him at all. Well, it's more than that. I think she tries to avoid spending time with him if she can."

"Have you ever met him?"

"No, when he comes down here, he usually calls her to meet him someplace. I don't know that he's ever come to the school. Or if he has, I've never seen him."

"Has she said why she doesn't like spending time with him?"

"Yeah, she's talked to me and Denise a couple of times." George leaned forward, his elbows on Malcolm's desk. "She says she barely knows him and he wasn't around much when she was growing up. Her grandparents and her mother never had much to say about him. That's weird, isn't it? I guess they didn't like him. She said one time she didn't know why her mother married him. Denise said that can happen sometimes, people make you think they are different from who they really are."

"I'm sure that's true," Malcolm said. "What else has she said about him?"

"When she first came to Cincinnati, she lived with him in Dayton for a few weeks, but she didn't enjoy it." George sat back in his chair. "When she's been at his house, she says sometimes there are people who come by to talk to him. They always go into his study and shut the door. But she says those people are really creepy and make her uncomfortable. She says some of them are a little scary."

Malcolm leaned forward. "Did she mention anything specific?"

"Gloria didn't like telling me this, but she said one man borrowed a book from her father. She got a look at the title. It was Adolph Hitler's book, *Mein Kampf*."

"I can understand why she didn't want to tell you that."

"And she said a couple of men came by one time and dropped off bags that had leaflets in them. Her father locked them away in a closet, so she didn't know what they were. She also told me…and she didn't want me to say anything to Denise…that she had never mentioned she and Denise are friends, because she knows her father wouldn't like it."

"She thinks he a racist."

"Yeah, she does. I get the feeling she only visits him because she thinks since he's her father she owes him that. After all, he gave her a car, and she likes having it." He paused for a moment before continuing. "She's a really great girl, Lieutenant Mitchell. She and Denise are very good friends, and Gloria and I get along fine. I wonder if her parents broke up because of her father's political views? Gloria sure doesn't share them."

"Thank you, George. You've been a great help." Malcolm stood and extended his hand. "Please remember this conversation doesn't leave this room."

"Roger that, Lieutenant Mitchell. If I think of anything else, or hear anything else, I'll call you."

***

Malcolm recounted the gist of this conversation at dinner, as they enjoyed the delectable meal Milly and Augusta had prepared.

"This is great. What did you say it is?" He asked Milly.

"Creamy Tuscan Chicken Pasta," Milly replied. "And now your wife has the recipe."

"Getting back to your interview with George...," Augusta prompted.

"My take is that Rodgers has been pretty open with his daughter regarding his racism, and she's afraid to disagree with him."

"I understand he's not paying for her college expenses," Garrett commented. "She doesn't owe him anything, as far as I can tell. Probably just a misplaced sense of familial duty."

"George says he shows up unexpectedly from time to time and takes Gloria to dinner. And my guess is she's afraid to refuse him." Mal took his last bite of Italian food and swallowed half a glass of water.

"About Gloria being Gardner instead of Rodgers. Garrett helped us with that." Mal lifted his glass to his friend.

"I contacted a criminal attorney I went to law school with who is now in Montgomery," Garrett told them. "He did a little digging and found that after the divorce, Gloria's mother petitioned the court to legally resume her maiden name. Since her mother had primary custody, the judge—who happened to be a family friend—also changed Gloria's name." He lifted an eyebrow. "Which no doubt at least annoyed Ben Rodgers."

"It sounds as though Gloria and George have become pretty close friends," Milly remarked.

"In fact, it's Denise James and Gloria who are close," Mal said. "George is peripheral."

"Benjamin Rodgers can't be too thrilled about that friendship," Augusta said. "If Gloria even told him about it."

"George said she has not." Mal drained his water glass.

One more piece of information. When Gloria first came to Ohio, she lived with Rodgers in Dayton for a couple of months before school started. That's when he bought the car and saw to it she got an Ohio license."

"So where are you now with a possible warrant to search his property?" Garrett asked.

"Waiting to hear back from my friend at the DPD about what he's learned from the beat cops on Rodgers' street. If we know he wasn't home last night, that should give us the last piece of ammunition we need."

Mal and Garrett took Fritz for a final walk as the women cleared the table and cleaned up the kitchen, putting away leftovers.

"When this is over, you and I are going to take Fritz for a walk while the men do K.P.," Augusta remarked.

"The nice thing about that plan is they won't hesitate to agree. We're pretty lucky ladies with the men in our lives," Milly said.

"That we are," Augusta agreed. "Poor Gloria. What's going to happen with her, do you think? She's going to learn that her father is a lot more than a bigot and a strange person. He's a murderer, and once he's

247

arrested, he'll probably go to jail for life. Her family is hundreds of miles away. They may want her to come back to Montgomery."

Milly placed the few leftovers in the refrigerator. "You're talking about her kin. Not necessarily her family. She's building her true family right here. Claudia, George, Denise, and probably other people as well. If you remember, you and I did exactly the same thing when we were students here."

"You're absolutely right. I will always love my Uncle Lenny…he's my kin. And of course, Mal and his boys and their families are mine now. But my family is much broader. You, Garrett, Dennis Halloran, John Edmanston…just to name a few. And my students."

Mal and Garrett hadn't been back inside for more than a few minutes before Mal's phone in the alcove rang. He closed the door in order to keep his conversation private as Milly and Augusta played fetch with Fritz in the living room. Garrett sat at the piano, picking out a melody with two fingers.

"I've offered to give you lessons," Milly told him.

"Why do I need to learn to play the piano? My lady is one of the greatest concert pianists on the planet." A few more plunks. "I'm just taking up time until Malcolm tells us what's going on. This is a nasty situation."

Mal had on what Augusta thought of as his "full detective face" when he opened the door—set jaw, narrowed eyes. "Bad news. Benjamin Rodgers' whereabouts are unknown. Neither Rodgers nor his car have been seen in over twenty-four hours. None of his neighbors have seen him. The cops checked his printing shop and there's a notice on the door, 'Closed Until Further Notice.'"

So, it's entirely possible he was here in Cincinnati last night and put an explosive device in Milly's car," Augusta said.

"He could be anywhere," Garrett said. "He might even be back in Alabama, though that seems like a bad move. Or in Canada, which would be smarter. What's the next move, Lieutenant Mitchell?"

"Detective Keenhold agreed to put out an APB on Rodgers' car, and Garrett is right, he could be anywhere. 'In the wind' is an apt description in this case. He may be in hiding somewhere. He has to know his attempt to bomb Milly's car failed since there was nothing in the news about it this morning. He could be running scared."

"Do you need to go to Dayton?" Augusta asked. *Please say no. I want you to stay here. I have a bad feeling about this.*

"There's really nothing more I could do there at this point. We're coordinating with the DPD. I'll talk to Jim and Dan when they relieve the other detectives at midnight; they may have heard something. Rodgers looks guilty as hell." Mal glanced at each of them.

"One more thing: I'm taking steps to secure a warrant to search Rodgers' house in the morning. And also his print shop. It'll be interesting to see what we find."

"Well, bomb-making materials sound like a good possibility," Augusta said. "But you still don't really have much evidence that would point to him being Gene Geller's killer."

"No, we don't. If we find him and question him, our best bet would be a confession. I doubt Rodgers would do that unless our search turns up something." He sank down on the sofa. "If Rodgers somehow nabbed Geller during the Avondale riot, I'd sure like to know how he managed that."

"It's not even nine o'clock," Garrett said as he stood. "It's going to be a long night, but there's some great mindless television on. 'Green Acres' and then 'Gomer Pyle.' What do you say, Madame Peerless Pianist? Want to zone out in front of the TV with me in the guest bedroom?"

"Absolutely. I'm exhausted. It's been a very long day as well." They said their goodnights.

Augusta stood, stretched, and yawned. "I'm with Milly. It's been a long, stressful day and evening, and I'd love to close my eyes. I know you're planning to talk to Jim and Danny…but they won't be here for another…," she checked her watch, "…two hours and forty minutes."

"I'm not interested in mindless television, bride, but I wouldn't mind stretching out for a bit if that would help you get to sleep." He stood and wrapped an arm around her.

"I'd like that, Lieutenant Mitchell. I always feel safe when you're next to me." She hesitated. "Mal…is the reason you're not leaving because you think there's a chance Rodgers might show up here?'

He gazed at her for a long moment. "Augusta, I don't know what Rodgers is capable of. I don't like to think that could happen, but I can't dismiss it. I have to be honest with you." He pulled her close. "I think it's a good thing that there are three law enforcement officers on this property tonight."

***

After changing into sweats, Malcolm held Augusta in his arms until she drifted off to sleep, Fritz right next to his side of the bed. Mal gazed at his sleeping wife, glad to see her finally relaxed.

This was different from Augusta's earlier encounters with danger. She'd even kept her cool during the awful time she had been held captive for days, facing her enemy, outwitting him. But Malcolm was aware of the anxiety she had struggled to control since her terrifying experience of handling a car with no brakes— only to learn later they had been deliberately disabled.

This was different. First the anonymous threats, then hang-up calls, and now twice attempts on her life from an unknown, faceless enemy. *Now, at least, we believe we know who it is.*

Malcolm hadn't shared with her, or Garrett and Milly, that his earlier private phone conversations included a call to his son, letting Dan know he sensed that Benjamin Rodgers had been stalking Augusta, and no doubt knew where they lived.

"Now that he's in the wind, I have a gut feeling he may try something tonight," he told Danny. "I need you to go to the station before you come here and get three of the portable radios. Come a little earlier than midnight, maybe eleven-thirty? I'll meet you at your car and bring one inside. I won't be sleeping, and I'll have Fritz right next to me. I'll be on Channel 1, but don't key up unless there's a reason. I don't want to wake Gus unless and until it's necessary."

The CPD had just begun to use these radio units, sometimes called walkie-talkies, after trying them out a couple of years earlier. They were clunky and large, built to military specifications, but they had proved useful on more than one case. Mal was sure being able to immediately communicate with Dan and Jim would be vital if Rodgers did show up. *A dumb move if he does try it, but the man's a psychopath. I'm convinced he murdered Eugene Geller and thinks he's gotten away with it. And Gus is his unfinished business.*

At eleven-thirty Malcolm carefully disentangled himself from Augusta and moved quietly to the window, watching the car with Dan and Jim pull up the curved driveway and park in the driveway extension on the side of the house, where they could see part of the back of the property as well as the front. They would take turns circling the house on foot every half hour. Mal attached Fritz's leash and took him along as he soundlessly went downstairs and outside to collect his portable radio.

The rain had stopped earlier, and now clouds scudded across the crescent moon.

"I may be wrong about this, but I'm convinced Rodgers killed Eugene Geller. And he's twice attempted to murder my wife. We know he's not in Dayton. He could show up here. When you check the house, no flashlights tonight."

"You think he's lost his mind," Jim said.

"He lost it a long time ago. No telling what he might try."

Mal returned to his bedroom and found Augusta continuing to sleep peacefully. *I can't lose her. She's my life.* He took off his slippers and carefully eased himself onto the bed. Staying awake was not a problem for a detective who had many experiences with stakeouts in his history.

Two o'clock. Fritz sat up abruptly, a low growl in his throat. Seconds later, a signal from the radio. Mal laid gentle fingers on Augusta's lips, whispering calmly into her ear, "Don't make a sound. We may have something going on here."

Augusta's eyes flashed open with fear. She nodded, clutching the covers tightly to her chest.

"Mitchell. Over."

"We have a visitor in the back," Dan informed him. "How do you want to handle this? Over."

"I'm coming downstairs. When I flip on the outside light, turn on your headlights. We'll all three have guns on him. Then follow my lead. Over and out."

"Stay here, and keep Fritz with you," he told Augusta, shoving his feet into slippers. He slung the walkie-talkie over one shoulder by a strap, grabbed his gun from the chiffonier, and rushed downstairs to the back door.

Peering through the back door window, Malcolm became aware of a shadow, then the outline of a man with a box under one arm moving cautiously toward the house. Rage raced through him. *Don't lose it, Mitchell.*

In one swift movement, Malcolm opened the kitchen door, flipped on the outside light above the door with his left hand, pushed open the screen door with his right shoulder, stepped out, and had his gun pointed at Rodgers—as if he had practiced this exact choreography thousands of times. Simultaneously, the detectives' car lights came on and Jim and Dan jumped out and ran to the back of the house, guns drawn.

"Put the package down! Put the package down!" Malcolm roared, the command echoed by the two detectives.

Caught completely off guard, Rodgers froze in his tracks, stared at Malcolm advancing toward him...and slowly obeyed, his hands shaking.

Malcolm barked, "Put your hands on top of your head and interlock your fingers! Kneel down!"

Rodgers hesitated.

"*I said kneel down*!"

This achieved the desired result.

"Jim, you search him. I'd break something," Malcolm commanded through clenched teeth, sidling to the left. "Danny, spread right."

Jim grabbed Rodgers' fingers hard, preventing him from pulling them apart. With his right hand, he patted Rodgers down on the right, right front, and right rear. He changed hands and did the same on Rodgers' left, extracting a revolver from his belt.

"Rodgers! What in God's name were you thinking?" Jim yelled. "The Chief of Detectives' *wife*?" Jim roughly pulled Rodgers' hands behind his back. "You're under arrest for attempted murder."

254

With three law enforcement officers surrounding him, a totally cowed Benjamin Rodgers stared at the ground.

Moving carefully, Jim took the box a distance from the house and opened it. "A pipe bomb. Same as the one I found in Milly's car. It hasn't been armed."

Mal lowered his gun. "Your collar, Detective Edmonds." The rage returned. "Get this obnoxious pile of odiferous fecal matter off my property."

Chapter 23
Sarastro Prevails

Augusta lay still for a moment, turning over in her mind the conversation she'd heard between Malcolm and Danny. *When did he get the portable radio? I didn't see it earlier.*

"*Mitchell. Over.*"

"*We have a visitor at the back. How do you want to handle this? Over.*"

"*I'm coming downstairs. When I flip on the outside light, turn on your headlights. We'll all three have guns on him. Then follow my lead. Over and out.*"

Fritz, his jowls resting on the bed next to her, whined softly. Augusta took a deep breath, patted Fritz, and slid out of bed, throwing on a robe. It seemed that mere seconds had passed when she became aware of light coming from below through the side window of the bedroom, and she heard men shouting.

Augusta flew down the hall, Fritz at her heels, to see Garrett and Milly coming through the guest bedroom door. She ran past them and down the steps, heading toward the back door.

It was ajar, and once she reached it, she could hear more clearly. Augusta hesitated, knowing instinctively not to go outside, but she was able to see enough to realize Mal and the two detectives had apprehended a trespasser in their backyard. Heart pounding, she kept a hand on Fritz's collar and quieted him when she heard the growl in his throat.

Aware of Milly and Garrett standing close behind her, Augusta pushed the door open a few more inches. A man knelt on the ground, hands on head, and she heard Jim yell something at him as he held up an object. *A gun?*

More lights…this time flashing red lights from two silent patrol cars as they pulled up to the house. *Jim and Dan must have called for backup.*

Augusta stepped close to the door, pushing it open still further, and she now had a better view of the man's face. His eyes were on the ground, but he glanced up and glared at her murderously. She felt a flutter in her stomach but lifted her chin and returned the stare. *Just as Mal suspected, Benjamin Rodgers had the audacity to come to our home.* He was no longer the rather nice-looking man she had seen in the mug shot. Augusta now saw him for what he was—the face of evil. The life of hatred he had chosen distorted him, both inwardly and outwardly.

Mal crossed to speak to the cops and Augusta watched as Jim handcuffed the intruder. One of the patrolmen came across the yard and picked up a small box as Jim hustled his captive toward the car. Malcolm handed his portable radio to Dan, and all three police cars headed out.

He strode across the yard to the back door, reaching for it just as Augusta opened it for him. They moved into each other's arms, holding each other tightly for a long moment.

Glancing at Milly and Garrett, Mal said, "Show's over, folks. Let's get inside and I'll let you know what happened out here."

Milly grabbed wine glasses and a bottle of merlot as they settled in the living room, Augusta, her heart still racing, on the sofa close to Malcolm, Fritz lying at his feet. He recounted exactly what had happened, beginning with the conversation he'd had with Jim and Dan earlier that evening.

Augusta gazed at her hero husband, aware of his emotions as she recalled him telling her not long after they met of the enormous satisfaction he received after apprehending a killer. *"The endorphins scatter in your brain like fireworks. It may be the best thing you ever feel."* She had been tempted to ask, *"Better than sex?"* but refrained.

Mal completed his story, telling them he'd had a feeling Rodgers might show up at their house, which is why he called Danny and told him to pick up the portable radios before they came to handle the midnight-to-eight detail.

"No surprise that. Malcolm Mitchell gets his man, once again. Only this time it got far too personal."

Garrett drained his wine glass. "Well, I'm for going back to bed and getting a few more hours of sleep. Congratulations…Chief."

He stood, holding out a hand to Milly. "Coming, my lady?"

"I'll rinse these out when we get up," Milly said, placing the glasses on a tray. "Sleep sounds excellent to me. But we'll have plenty more to talk about later this morning." They headed upstairs.

Augusta gazed at Malcolm. "So it's over?"

"Almost. Rodgers is guilty of at least two counts of attempted murder. Somewhere in his house or that shop he operates I believe I'll find something that conclusively ties him to Geller's murder as well."

She leaned toward him. "My magnificent love. My hero. You look…," she searched for a word. "Victorious."

"Remember what I told you about the feeling I get when we catch the bad guy?"

"You mean about the endorphins popping. I certainly do."

A look passed between them.

"You should go back to bed, Gus."

"I'm not at all sleepy, Mal. In fact, I'm wide awake. Too much adrenalin."

A grin. "Adrenalin or endorphins?"

Augusta jumped up and headed for the stairs. "Maybe both."

After a quick command to Fritz to "stay," Malcolm followed and moved ahead of her. He grasped one of her hands and went up the steps two at a time, both of them stifling their laughter as he pulled Augusta along until they reached the top, where he picked her up and carried her into their bedroom.

***

Now that Rodgers was safely in jail, the protective detail was withdrawn and both Augusta and Milly were able to return to their normal lives. Garrett drove them to the Conservatory once they were up and about. Nothing had appeared as yet in the news about what happened on Vista Circle Wednesday night, but it was sure to break later that day.

Augusta wasn't surprised to receive a phone call from *The Morning Call*'s reporter Arnold Richter, a person with whom she had a sometimes contentious, sometimes cordial relationship.

"You know I can't tell you anything until the police hold a press conference, Arnie."

"Not even if I cross my heart and swear I won't say a word until that happens? Come on, Augusta. I think you owe me one after I did you a big favor last year when your kid George Van Dorn was being held hostage."

"Lieutenant Mitchell would be very upset with me, Arnie. I'm sorry, but once that press conference is held, I'll fill you in however I can. I'll give you an exclusive interview, in fact."

Malcolm called her later. "Rodgers' property was a gold mine. We found all the evidence we need to charge him with attempted murder of you and Milly. His

261

basement was full of everything he needed to build more bombs."

"Just as you expected."

"Yes, but we had a huge bonus. In a safe in his so-called 'publishing company' we found a large mailing envelope marked 'June 12, 1967.' Want to guess what was in it?"

"Gene Geller's wallet?"

"Yep."

"Good lord, Malcolm. He kept it as a souvenir."

"Right on, Detective McKee-Mitchell, and he also kept Geller's car keys. The wallet contained four hundred dollars in cash and of course Geller's driver's license and his charge card. Nothing had been removed." He paused for a moment. "But get this. There were other wallets and sets of keys—four of them, in fact. None from Cincinnati, but other cities in Southern Ohio. Two from Dayton. Keenhold has all of that and mentioned a couple of unsolved murders over the past six or so years."

Augusta gripped the phone. "Dear God. Are you saying the man may have been a serial killer?"

"I don't want to speculate; that remains to be seen. For the present, he's our prisoner, in our jurisdiction, and I'm focusing on the Geller murder."

"That's what you've been working for this entire time. Justice for Eugene Geller. Next you interview Rodgers and let him know you have him dead to rights. And hope he'll fill in some blanks for you," Augusta guessed.

"Yes, such as how he managed to abduct Geller and get him out of Avondale, and how Geller's car ended up at that house in Mt. Healthy. Oh, and in a desk in his house, we found the sales record for a second car...a 1959 Chevy, purchased and registered in Alabama. Our men are checking around our neighborhood to see if it's parked there. I'm sure it is."

"Where's the Porsche?"

"Just a guess, but I would bet it's sitting in a private parking garage somewhere in or near Dayton. My theory is that he rented space and switched cars when he made his little excursions. Which could very well include the owners of those other driver's licenses we found."

"Oh, Malcolm. I hate to think what he might have done, perhaps to Elena or her children, if you hadn't stopped him. He's insane."

"Probably. But if there's any spark of humanity left in him, he'll confess to what he's done and spare his daughter the agony of a trial. And when he hears what we have, that might happen."

"I'll pray that it does." She shifted in her chair. "Mal...George Van Horn will be here in about ten minutes for a lesson. Can I thank him for his help?"

"Yes, you can do that. Only don't tell him anything. He's already worried about Gloria, though, he told me that yesterday. He suspects her father is the reason you've been under police protection."

"George is smart. When he sees I'm back teaching he'll know the danger has been removed."

"If he says that, you can confirm it, and tell him we'll have a press conference later today and then he'll know more."

Augusta stood and moved around her desk, leaning against it. "Arnie Richter called me."

"Imagine that. He wants to interview you, doesn't he? After the press conference, I would hope."

"I owe him, Mal. If it weren't for his help, we might have never rescued George last year."

"True." A pause. "Okay, fine. I will never like the guy. But he's a good reporter, and I respect that."

Augusta laughed. "I'm so relieved this is over. My biggest concern right now is Gloria. I wish she could be spared this horror. How will she react to finding out her father is a killer? She's going to be...I can't even imagine."

***

Augusta and Milly met in the faculty lounge to watch the press conference. Chief Jake Schott made the announcement that Benjamin Rodgers, a resident of Dayton, had been arrested for the murder of Eugene Geller. He then commented that Rodgers' arrest came about partly as a result of the investigation into more than one attempt on the life of Augusta McKee Mitchell, the wife of Cincinnati's Chief of Detectives, and that Rodgers was also being charged with her attempted homicide.

"Rodgers has made a full confession," Chief Schott concluded. "He will be arraigned and will be transferred to the Hamilton County Jail in the next few days."

Immediately the reporters started shouting questions: "When did he try to kill Mrs. Mitchell?"…"What can you tell us about the attempts on Mrs. Mitchell's life?"…"Has he been living right here in Cincinnati?"

The Chief answered the last question, saying that Rodgers had been residing in Dayton for the past eight years, which created an even bigger din.

"What was he doing there?"…"Has he made attempts on other people's lives?"…"Who else could he have murdered?"

"Feeding frenzy," Milly murmured.

"Just doing their jobs," Augusta commented, a wry grin tugging at her lips. "I'm so glad this is over."

"Aren't we all? Now you can get back to Mozart's fantasy world," Milly said.

***

Over a dinner of leftovers from the night before, Malcolm told Augusta more.

"It didn't take him but a couple of minutes to decide to confess once we told him what we had found. Good God, the madness that spewed from that man's mouth! He hated you for considering casting Black students for your opera, even after he sent you notes warning you not to…and especially when you cast a Black girl in the lead role he thought his daughter should have."

265

"And that's why he wanted me dead?" Augusta shook her head in disbelief.

Mal hesitated a moment before he spoke. "He wouldn't admit to being given a directive from the KKK to…remove you, but he said this: 'Your wife is a large part of what's wrong with America—race traitors.'"

Augusta abruptly put her fork down and stared at her husband. "He actually said that?"

"It's part of the indoctrination of the organization, I believe. I'm sorry, Gus. Maybe I shouldn't have told you."

"No, I think I needed to hear it." A sigh. "It's frightening."

Malcolm leaned across the table and took both her hands as they sat quietly for a moment.

"One good thing…Rodgers also said he didn't want his daughter to have to endure being around for a trial, he says he's going to plead guilty. So that spark of humanity may exist. Chances are there will be a trial, though. Rodgers' attorney will insist on it, and when Rodgers has time to think about the fact he's facing electrocution, he may change his mind."

"Yes, I've heard Garrett talk about the way the system works often enough to realize that's likely the case. I'd think Rodgers' attorneys might have him plead insanity."

Malcolm again reached over and covered her hand with his. "Gus, your hunch about Gloria being Rodgers' daughter was invaluable. It literally blew both cases wide open—Eugene Geller's murder and the attempts on your life. I wish I could pin a medal on you."

Augusta gazed at the man she adored and squeezed his hand. "I feel as if you just did."

After a moment, they resumed their meal. Augusta sighed as she said, "Poor Gloria. George told me his parents want her to think of them as family, and they've invited her to stay with them. Apparently, Gloria and George's mother really hit it off. That's comforting."

Mal nodded. "That is a good thing." A final bite of chicken. "Oh, and I was right about the cars. The Chevy was found parked about three blocks away from our place. You know that empty house on Vista Avenue?"

"Yes, I know the house you mean." She folded her napkin. "How did he know to park there?"

"This won't be easy for you to hear." Mal took a swig of beer. "He stalked you for weeks. That's how he knew your car. And he cased our neighborhood several times, usually late at night." He wiped his mouth.

"Sooner or later, you're going to ask me this, so I might as well tell you now. The bomb he had on him last night...he planned to rig it so that it would detonate when the back door was opened. He didn't care who was killed. Whatever happened, your life would be changed forever."

Augusta stared at him, unable to speak for a few minutes. "I saw Rodgers last night for exactly who he is, and you just confirmed that with what he said about me in your interview. He sees himself as some kind of crusader, attempting to change the world to fit his vision. He's a destroyer. A little like Mozart's Queen of the Night. And unfortunately, he's not alone."

Mal put his fork down and gazed at her. "You could be right."

They sat silently for a few moments. Augusta asked, "Did he ever actually work at a job? And what did he do?"

"He didn't do much in that so-called printing house of his. It was mainly a front for the KKK to pass propaganda through. Rodgers had inherited some money and invested it. That was his main source of income."

Mal leaned back. "He answered all my questions about Geller's murder, too. Rodgers had stalking people down to an art, which is why you were never aware of him targeting you. He'd stalked Gene and knew everything about his routine. He knew when Geller spent time at Rockdale Temple. He even knew where Gene parked his car when he was there."

Another swig of beer. "Rodgers followed the news about all the racial unrest in Cincinnati and heard from his KKK pals that the rally in Avondale that day might turn into a riot. He thought that might be his chance to get Gene. He wanted to go down there and 'join the party' anyway…his words. I asked him if he was the one who threw the brick through the store window that started the riot. He halfway smiled and said, 'Maybe.'"

Augusta shuddered. "Go on."

"That evening he followed Geller when he left the Temple with the kids and then when Gene went to his car Rodgers struck him hard in the back of his head with a steel blackjack—which, by the way, is at the bottom of the Great Miami River somewhere. Then he stuffed Geller into the trunk of the car and drove it deep into the woods. He'd already scoped out a spot where a body would likely never be found."

Mal paused. "This shows how ruthless the guy is. Just for good measure, he found a heavy rock and struck Geller's head again."

"Why on earth would he do that?" Augusta asked, horrified.

"I asked the same question. He said to obliterate the mark from the blackjack wound, just in case the body was found. After he dumped Geller's body, he took the car through a car wash and drove it to Mt. Healthy."

"Which is where he had his own car parked, as you suspected."

"Exactly. Rodgers had parked his Chevy in a lot in Mt. Healthy and took public transportation to Avondale. Then after he dumped the body and did the car wash, he parked Geller's car on the outskirts of Mt. Healthy. He'd been there the day before and found a house which appeared to be abandoned, and he left Geller's car there. He then walked to the parking lot and retrieved his Chevy. He always put the Porsche in the rental garage and used the '49 Chevy for his 'missions.' Rodgers made sure people connected him to the Porsche, which is the reason he parked it in front of his house."

"But how did he know Gene would be at Rockdale Temple that night? He usually was there only when there were services."

"Rodgers was nothing if not thorough. At some point he had the name and address of his printing shop added to the Temple's mailing list. The confirmation rehearsal and Geller's role in it was announced the week before in their newsletter."

"So that's the how," Augusta said. "But did Rodgers tell you why?"

"He called Gene 'the devil incarnate' who held his darling Elena in a spell all these years, and…get this…he said he plans to 'win her back' when this is all over. So, it was exactly what Titus Powlett first told you. Unrequited love. And undying hate. He never got over Elena rejecting him for Gene…who was a Jew."

Chapter 24
Thanksgiving

Thanksgiving dawned bright and clear. Two weeks had passed since Benjamin Rodgers had been put away, hopefully for good. It took a while for Augusta to overcome the lingering fear Rodgers had created in her, but with Mal's loving concern and support, Augusta found herself thinking less about her distressing experience. Instead, she focused on the many good things in her life: family, friends, her students, and the upcoming opera production. And most of all, music—taking to heart the advice she had given Allan Meissner, immersing herself in the music that filled her life and letting it renew her spirit.

She let Malcolm sleep in and took Fritz for his morning walk, enjoying the brisk air. After giving Fritz water and a toy to gnaw on, she went into the kitchen to prepare a breakfast tray for her husband. *He does this so often for me. I should do it more for him.*

Augusta snatched up the phone on the first ring in hopes of it not waking Malcolm and heard Letitia Van

Dorn's voice. "I hope this isn't too early, but it's the first chance I've had to call you. You know Gloria's been staying here."

"Yes, George told me. I know it's been a great help to her. You've made her part of your family."

"She fits right in, Augusta. We love having her here. And late yesterday her grandparents arrived to spend Thanksgiving with us."

"I had no idea you invited them. What a generous thing for you to do, Letitia. I hope it's working out well."

"They're absolutely wonderful people. You know, except for the accent, it's kind of hard to believe they're from Montgomery. They could be from right here in Cincinnati. I hope at some point you get to meet them. Barbara—Gloria's grandmother—in some ways reminds me of you. She's a successful attorney who tackles some tough issues in her practice. And it's easy to understand why she's so forward-thinking when you talk to Gloria's grandfather, Tim, another attorney. As a matter of fact, they're in practice together."

"How is Gloria doing? I know learning about her father's crimes had to be difficult."

"Yes, it was dreadful for her. At first, she kept apologizing…as if any of it was that sweet girl's fault. She doesn't like to talk about him, and she made it clear she has no intention of visiting him in jail. Your cast of *The Magic Flute* really embraced her, though. She's been surrounded by loving support from her Conservatory friends, and overall, she's doing pretty well. Better than I would, I think."

"Well, I appreciate how much you and your family are doing to help her," Augusta said. "Have a wonderful holiday. Let's get together sometime over winter break, shall we?"

"I was about to say that exact same thing," Letitia trilled. "Have a wonderful time with your family and hug that precious grandbaby for me, will you?"

She paused. "One more thing…did I tell you I think you made the perfect choice for the spring production? I believe your audiences will love *The Magic Flute*, such a beautiful fairy tale. But there's a lot more to it than that, and I also feel it may make some people think. It helps people look for the good in the world."

Wonder if Wolfgang would have approved? Augusta thought as she hung up the phone. *Is this why he wrote it, to help people find their way to peace and harmony? Maybe it is.*

Since Mal's ex-wife Carla insisted on having "my" family for Thanksgiving dinner, Malcolm and Augusta usually waited until the weekend after the holiday to celebrate with his sons and their wives. But this year Carla and her husband were off on a cruise, and Dan's Martha had asked to host Thanksgiving. Her invitation included Milly and Garrett since both of Mal's sons and their wives considered them family.

Augusta and Lacey had spent most of Wednesday afternoon helping Martha prepare for their feast. Fritz was invited to join them, and they all enjoyed watching baby Max with the big dog. Max had progressed to rocking back and forth on his hands and knees, getting ready to crawl, and Fritz lay next to his best friend, unblinking eyes fixed on the baby, one ear perked up to catch any threatening sounds. *The best bodyguard Maxie could possibly have,* Augusta thought.

Fritz, as good a dog as he was, was not invited the following day, but Augusta patted his head and promised to bring him some turkey from dinner.

"Why do you do that? Hand feeding him again," Mal said, fastening his seat belt.

"He looked so sad. He knows we're about to have a great time and wishes he could go."

Malcolm grinned at her. "You are such a softie. When did you turn into such a sappy doggie mom, anyway?"

"I think when I saw you down on the ground the day I gave Fritz to you and realized it was one of the best things I've ever done. You were like a little kid."

Malcolm gazed at her again, the shine in his intense blue eyes turning Augusta's insides to mush. "My wonderful bride. I don't think you know how much I love you, Gus."

She kissed him softly. "I know how much I love you. Before I met you, I had decided I'd never marry but would spend my life alone, teaching as long as I could and thinking of my students as my children. I thought that would be enough. Now here we are with a grandson, and no doubt more babies to come. What a wonderful life you've given me."

Malcolm returned the kiss, his lips lingering on hers. "Let's not stay out too late. I have plans for when we get back."

"Oh, good. I like the sound of that. Your plans are usually extremely satisfying."

"I aim to please," Mal laughed, and gave her a hug before turning on the ignition.

***

Their Thanksgiving gathering was everything Martha had hoped for, with an abundance of food, laughter, and love. Max, overstimulated by being passed from person to person, grew cranky and Mal took him upstairs to put him into his crib. Augusta waited for a few minutes and then followed quietly, peering through the door to the baby's room to see her homicide detective husband rocking Max in his arms and singing to him.

Singing? Mal is singing. I knew he sang in his high school chorus, but I've never heard him. In a pleasing baritone voice, Mal sang softly the Brahms Lullaby, sometimes filling in for words he didn't know with "la la la." Augusta watched as he tenderly placed Max in his crib and tucked covers around him, placing his favorite stuffed animals close by. Not wanting to startle the devoted grandfather, Augusta slipped down the stairs before Mal saw her.

She couldn't resist, though, humming the Brahms song as they drove home. Mal chuckled. "Now I wonder why you're singing that? Were you spying on me, bride?"

"One of the sweetest moments I've ever witnessed," Augusta said. "I love that you were singing to Max. One of these days I might even get you to sing with me. How about some lessons? I don't teach on Saturdays."

"You know…maybe after I retire, I'll take you up on that. But only if you guarantee you can train me well enough to perform the role of Scarpia in *Tosca*."

"That I can't promise, my love. But what a beautiful Thanksgiving this has been. Hearing you sing to Max was certainly a special moment." She unfastened her seat belt and slid closer to him, and he draped an arm around her.

If only this peace could last, Augusta thought. *But these are turbulent times, and I must accept that there will undoubtedly be more trouble in the future.*

She also knew that Malcolm would be involved in some intense—and possibly dangerous—situations during these difficult times, and she was aware that cops are human and make mistakes. Some make bad mistakes. *But in what other profession do they strap on a gun, pin on a badge, and leave their home day after day, knowing the day may come when they don't return? Far too many cops are killed in the line of duty. Please, not my cop. Keep him safe*

Mal tightened his arm around her, almost as if he were aware what she was thinking. She rested her head on his shoulder.

Live in the moment, Augusta. Be grateful for every good thing that comes your way.

***

276

Elena Geller had phoned Augusta not long after Rodgers' arrest to share her shock and dismay on learning Augusta had also been Rodgers' victim. She thanked Augusta profusely for her part in securing justice for her husband. "My children and I can finally move on, thanks to you and Lieutenant Mitchell," she said. Elena extended a personal invitation to Augusta and Malcolm to attend a memorial service being planned in her husband's honor.

The Saturday after Thanksgiving the service was held at Rockdale Temple—a celebration of Gene's life, not a funeral. Elena, Amanda, and all their children warmly greeted people as they entered the Temple.

Gene had made friends with members of the Black community in Avondale, taking part in community gatherings and patronizing Black-owned businesses, and their number among the attendees attested to the good will he had engendered. Family, friends, business associates, and the Jewish community of Cincinnati turned out in force to share this commemoration of his life. Despite his failings, Eugene Geller was a genuinely caring person whose loss would be felt by many.

Augusta glanced around at the huge gathering of the diverse members of the Cincinnati community who had come to pay their respects to the cantor. *I hope what I'm seeing right now is a glimpse into the future. Change may not come quickly, nor will it come easily.*

But I choose to believe it will come.

Acknowledgments

When I began writing the Augusta McKee mysteries, I chose to set the series in the city that owns a large piece of my heart. I spent sixteen happy years in Cincinnati, the Queen City. As a seventeen-year-old aspiring opera singer, I fell in love with this beautiful city of seven hills and its rich musical environment on my first visit to audition for the College-Conservatory of Music.

I arrived in September 1955 and spent my first years at the school, which at that time occupied a charming, compact campus in Mt. Auburn. Later, I lived in various areas of the city on both the "east" and "west" sides of town—native Cincinnatians let you know exactly where they are from; it's a friendly rivalry. I worked for a time in downtown Cincinnati and later spent several years on the staff of the Edgecliff Academy of Fine Arts at Edgecliff College, which became "Cliffside College" in the series.

Despite the charm which Cincinnati never lost for me, the 1960s were also a time of challenges in the United States. Cincinnati for the most part was peaceful, but by the later sixties, problems had definitely begun to surface. The riot which begins this book actually happened, and during that summer and the next, heightened societal tension was part of the climate. It was the Civil Rights era and there was a growing opposition to the war in Vietnam, as well as cultural experimentation in other ways.

Because of the escalating social unrest in the '60s, I had considered ending the Mckee "cozy" mystery series with *The Case of the Bogus Beatle.* Cozy mysteries typically portray an amateur sleuth solving murders in a small-town setting, and feature intrigue, suspense and misdirection, while avoiding gritty reality, profanity, graphic violence and sex, with an atmosphere that is light and somehow comforting rather than hard-boiled.

But after giving it more thought, it felt right to continue the series and incorporate the social issues into any additional novels. My more-than-editor Ashleigh Evans and I agreed the Augusta mysteries have not ever been "cozy" in the strictest sense: while Augusta is actively involved (sometimes more than she should be!) in each case, Malcolm and the police are tasked with bringing them to their conclusion; the stories take place in an urban setting, and because Augusta is a voice teacher, the plots largely unfold in the musical community. In promoting the books, I often refer to them as a (hashtag) musical murder mystery—so perhaps I've developed my own sub-genre?

Ashleigh Evan's input has been invaluable in many ways throughout this story, and I appreciate more than I can say her encouragement and support when more than once I was on the verge of throwing in the proverbial towel. (Spoiler alert!) She provided the idea for a key part of the plot, that the same man who killed the cantor was targeting Augusta. It was an inspiration.

Once again, retired Det. Lt. Stephen R. Kramer of the Cincinnati Police Division provided insight into basically all the "cop stuff" in this book—from formal police procedure to the importance of the beat cop for finding vital information about a suspect. Steve's thoughts guided me in developing the mindset of now Lieutenant Malcolm Mitchell, Chief of Detectives, and that assistance helped me bring those scenes more vividly to life.

I believe I need to thank one of my favorite composers, Wolfgang Amadeus Mozart, for his remarkable final opera *Die Zauberflöte*. It is one of the most popular operas in the world and one of the three most-performed. Mozart's music for this work is remarkable in that it contains a variety of styles, and even of different musical eras. I do wonder if Mozart had a premonition his life was nearing its end, and he left this work as a legacy not only musically, but to help us become more aware of the mysteries of the universe.

Friend and one-time theatrical colleague Kristopher Yoder, library director at the Trexler Masonic Library in Allentown, was kind enough to "vet" the comments about Freemasonry.

Thanks to Taylor von Kooten for another beautiful "Augusta McKee mystery" book cover. She has captured the spirit of the series with her remarkable designs.

Many thanks to my beta readers, whose input is extremely important. Michaele Benedict has generously been encouraging me since I first started on this writing journey in 2013, as has Eric Mark. Audrey Henry, Marti Lantz, Nate Taylor, and Ken Van Camp have also provided important feedback on all the mysteries as well as several of my other books. With this book in particular I am more grateful than they can know for their enthusiastic support.

And my thanks to the Lady Writers of the Poconos (also now known as the Shaggy Dog Productions Authors): Sahar Abdulaziz, Belinda Gordon, Evelyn Infante, Kelly Jennings, and Mary Ann Moore, for reading and responding to several sections from the book. Being a part of this group has been an important part of my professional growth, and we've developed warm friendships as well.

Finally, thanks to my characters. While I was discussing a book recently with a friend and fellow musician, he made the comment that I talk about my characters as if they are real people. My response? "They are real to me. If they were not, how could I make them real to a reader?"

Writing about social problems in the 1960s reinforced that those social issues are still with us all these years later, in the 2020s. And it is distressing to see the people of our country so divided on so many issues.

In the end, though, Augusta chooses to hope that change will come. I do as well.

Susan Moore Jordan
Pocono Mountains of Pennsylvania
May 2023

Videography

Avenu Malkeinu by Max Janowski
      Cantors Azi Schwartz, Shira Lissek, Rachel Brook
      Park Avenue Synagogue, New York

"The Doll Song"
      from *The Tales of Hoffmann* by Jacques
      Offenbach
      Carla Maffioletti, *soprano*
      André Rieu Orchestra

Selections from *Die Zauberföte* by W.A. Mozart
(sung in German)
      "Dies Bildnis"
      Fritz Wunderlich, *tenor*, as Tamino

      "Der Volgelfänger bin ich ja"
      Hermann Prey, *baritone*, as Papageno

      "Der Hölle Rache" (Vengeance Aria)
      Diana Damrau, *soprano,*
      as The Queen of the Night

      "Ach, ich fühl's"
      Kiri te Kanawa, *soprano*, as Pamina

      "In diesen heil'gen Hallen"
      Kurt Moll, *basso*, as Sarastro

"Soll ich dich, Teurer, nicht mehr sehn?"
Melissa Mino, *soprano*, as Pamina
Kwang Kyu Li, *basso*, as Sarastro
Pablo Henrich-Lobo, *tenor*, as Tamino

"Nur Stille, stille" – Act Two Finale
Metropolitan Opera, March 19, 2010
Ken Levine, Conductor

A complete performance of *The Magic Flute* in English
by Loyola University Of New Orleans (January, 2014)
is available on YouTube as of May, 2023

The Case of the Slain Soprano

(The Augusta McKee Mysteries, Book One)

Cincinnati, 1963: One-time opera singer Augusta McKee, professor of music on two college campuses, is successfully navigating her busy life in stiletto-shod feet—until she comes up against a shocking road block. Halfway through rehearsals for a production of "The Pirates of Penzance," Augusta receives the awful news that her leading lady has been murdered. But "the show must go on," and while forging ahead to make that happen, Augusta stumbles upon pertinent information which could lead to the identity of the perpetrator. First, though, Augusta must convince Homicide Detective Malcolm Mitchell that what she has uncovered can help him solve the case. While the strong-willed diva and the dashing detective clash at their first meeting, their dissonant chord becomes harmonious when Augusta and Malcolm continue to cross paths and discover a shared passion for opera ... and a strong desire to catch the killer.

THE CASE OF THE PURLOINED PROFESSOR

(The Augusta McKee Mysteries, Book Four)

Cincinnati, September 1964:

Aside from babysitting a colleague's rambunctious dog, life seems serene at the McKee home in Cincinnati—until Augusta's beau, Homicide Detective Malcolm Mitchell, receives a chilling phone call in the middle of the night from a mysterious crime kingpin. Midnight or not, friends and colleagues immediately convene. And within hours, the hunt for Augusta McKee—amateur sleuth, former opera singer and professor of music, last seen at a production staff meeting for her spring musical at Cliffside College—is on. Malcolm learns how perilous her situation is and what is being demanded in exchange for her safe return. He and his partner, Detective Jim Edmonds, muster their department's forces and assistance from the FBI as the danger mounts. To discover Augusta's location, Malcolm must piece together a trail of cryptic clues from Augusta herself. There is a deadline to meet, and time grows short. Where is Augusta? Can Malcolm find her in time to save her life? And can someone PLEASE stop that dog from barking?

THE CASE OF THE CHRYSANTHEMUM MURDERS

(The Augusta McKee Mysteries, Book Five)

Paris-Cincinnati, June 1965:

Augusta McKee, former opera singer and professor of music for two Cincinnati colleges, is enjoying her idyllic European honeymoon with Homicide Detective Malcolm Mitchell—until the day a fellow faculty member at the Conservatory of Music, a violinist and member of the Chrysanthemum String Quartet, is found dead in the same Paris hotel where they are staying. Within a week, a second member of the same quartet dies in Cincinnati under suspicious circumstances.

Malcolm, lead investigator in the case, and amateur sleuth Augusta learn of a mysterious cellist whose dismissal from the group might be grounds for revenge—except Anton Portnov died a year earlier in an automobile accident. Then there's the flamboyant local artist and mystery writer who hints at Portnov not being who he claimed to be; while at the same time, a lovely young usher at the Cincinnati Summer Opera—with a mysterious past of her own—shows an unusual interest in the quartet's new cellist.

Could either of these people be the killer?

Malcolm and Augusta find themselves on the case in this gripping international murder mystery—uncovering clues and searching for suspects before the Chrysanthemum String Quartet plays their final note.

The Cameron Saga

***

Memories of Jake

One brother can't remember. The other can't forget.

Andrew and Jacob Cameron are tied together by a bond more powerful than blood. As young children, they experience a horrific event that tears their family apart. Then just as they complete their high school years, the Vietnam War intensifies. Both young men serve in the military: Andrew in the Marine Corps, Jake as a Green Beret.

Each brother is damaged by his service in Vietnam, Jake in a way that will change his life forever. Andrew, always protective of his rakish younger brother, is determined to restore Jake and their relationship to normalcy. But when Jake disappears, Andrew's life is left in shambles.

His loving parents, his always supportive wife Mary, even his burgeoning career as an artist seem not to be enough to alleviate the pain of Andrew's frantic question:

Where is my brother?

Photo by Dr. Bertram Zarins.
Used by permission.

Man with No Yesterdays

'A thoughtful, superbly paced historical novel
looking at the emotional damage of war.
A FINALIST and highly recommended.'
The 2019 Wishing Shelf Book Awards
A SEMI-FINALIST IN THE
2020 KINDLE BOOK AWARDS
"A harrowing, humane, and inspiring book." - Dave Astor,
Literary Columnist

*"I was born somewhere over the South China Sea in a
military transport plane ..."*

Jake Cameron is facing the struggle of his life. A helicopter crash in Vietnam leaves Jake with total amnesia, and the young Green Beret returns home to a family he doesn't know and a life he can't remember.

Unable to be the son and brother his family has lost, Jake sets out to learn whatever he can about the man he was. When he uncovers a dark family secret, he decides to protect the people he loves by disappearing.

Susan Moore Jordan's new historical novel, MAN WITH NO YESTERDAYS, follows Jake on his journey as he fights to find himself ... a journey that takes him into his past, connects him with other Vietnam veterans, and eventually leads him to situations, places, and a love he would never have dreamed possible.

After a lifetime as a musician—performer, teacher, musical theater director—Susan Moore Jordan wrote and published her first novel in 2013 at the age of seventy-five, and she hasn't stopped since.

In her first four novels, the author drew from her life experiences as a voice teacher and stage director, and those historical novels were inspired by real people she encountered.

"Companion" novels, *Memories of Jake* and *Man with No Yesterdays* were released in 2017. A departure from her earlier historical novels, these two books detail the struggles of two brothers, Andrew and Jake Cameron, whose lives were irrevocably changed by their service in the Vietnam War. *Memories of Jake* was the recipient of an honorable mention Red Ribbon Award from the 2017 Wishing Shelf Book Awards. *Man With No Yesterdays* was a Finalist in the 2019 Wishing Shelf Book Awards.

Jordan next began "The Augusta McKee Mysteries." Book one, *The Case of the Slain Soprano*, was released in April, 2018 and *The Case of the Disappearing Director* followed in October, 2018. Additional books in the series followed, most recently Book #9, *The Case of the Casanova Cantor*. *The Case of the Slain Soprano* was a finalist in the 2018 Wishing Shelf Book Awards and a semi-finalist for the 2020 Kindle Book Awards. *The Case of the Disappearing Director* was a finalist in the 2019 Wishing Shelf Book Awards.

A third book in "The Cameron Saga," *And This Shall Be for Music*, was released in November of 2022. The book features the next generation of the family, Andrew's daughter Lindsey, an aspiring opera singer.

All of Jordan's books are "music-centric" (in the words of one reviewer), and readers comment on the strength of the element of music included in her work. Jordan sees writing as another way to share the music she loves, which she considers "the most powerful force in the universe."

Articles by Susan Moore Jordan have appeared in *Musical America* and *The Guardian*, and on August 2, 2019, she appeared on Hour Three of "The Today Show" as a Super Senior.

***

If you enjoyed
The Case of the Casanova Cantor,
please consider leaving a reader review from
whatever site you purchased the book.
Reviews are a standing ovation!
They are also valuable to indie authors
and greatly appreciated.
More information and links to all my books
can be found on my website,
www.susanmoorejordan.com